COLD HORROR FLOODED through Tyrell. *That injection was Hype. I have become an experimental animal.* The horror released the emotions he thought had been burned out of him by Jania's death. He rose from the examining table, forgetting his manacles. "You're out of your mind, you can't hand power like that over to the SIS!" The ankle chain caught on a projection and he pitched forward, hitting the ground hard in the heavy gravity. He looked up, spitting blood.

Morrow smiled again, looking down on him. "You are small minded, Mr. Tyrell. Timid in your thinking. The SIS is funding me, yes, but the government will never control time." He leaned closer. "*I* will."

MISSION CRITICAL™

DEATH OF THE PHOENIX

A NOVEL

PAUL C. CHAFE

PRIMA PUBLISHING

ISBN: 1-7615-0234-3
Library of Congress Catalog Card Number: 95-72402

Printed in the United States of America
96 97 98 99 EE 10 9 8 7 6 5 4 3 2 1

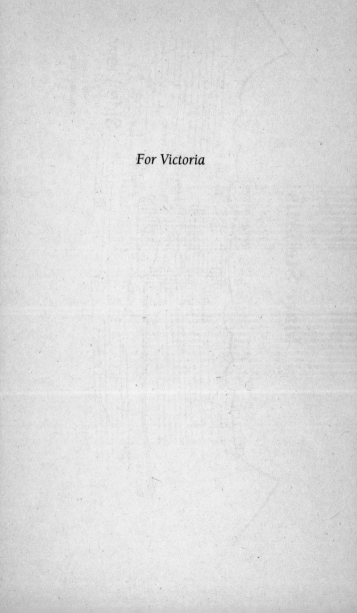

For Victoria

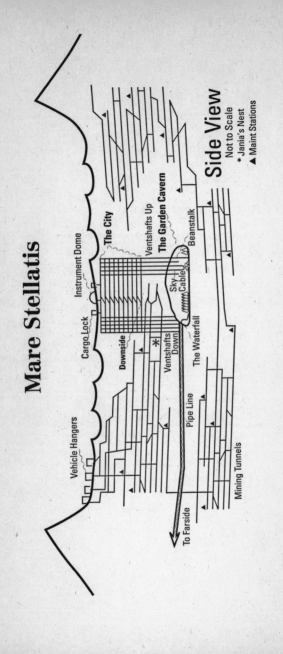

Mare Stellatis

Side View

Not to Scale

* Jania's Nest
▲ Maint Stations

Vehicle Hangers

Cargo Lock

Instrument Dome

The City

Downside

Ventshafts Up

The Garden Cavern

Beanstalk

Sky-Cable

Ventshafts Down

The Waterfall

Pipe Line

Mining Tunnels

To Farside

THE RISE AND FALL OF THE UNITED NATIONS

THE TWENTIETH CENTURY saw more human strife and progress than the previous thousand years. A scant lifetime separated the dawn of powered flight and the exploration of space—and the rate of advance increased exponentially and apparently without limit. There were limits of course, two of them. The first great limiting factor was the ratio of available raw resources to the total human population. The second was far more constricting and was defined by political willpower. During the twentieth century, the advance of the human race was driven hard up against those limits.

The god Technology had the power to ease those limits, but seldom without cost. For a time humanity hung poised between exaltation and destruction, the left and right hands of their god.

Always it offered the dream of utopia; always the dream hid nightmare realities. Limitless nuclear power brought indestructible nuclear waste. The vast yields of bioengineered crops crowded out natural biodiversity and brought the risk of devastating plagues. Extended life spans triggered the explosion of the population bomb. The information age empowered the individual—and handed the state tools of control that even gave dictators pause. There were those who sought to turn away, to solve human problems with simpler solutions. They were not wrong, but no one who chose that route could influence the course of global events—the genie could not be put back into the bottle. Power is the measure of a god, and technology is a powerful god by any measure. It rewarded its acolytes in gold and influence, and it rewarded most those who offered it the greatest tribute. Most people living in the twentieth century were all too ready to make sacrifices to technology's shrine. Most were not even aware they were doing it.

In the twenty-first century, civilization finally harnessed the rogue god and brought the four horsemen of the apocalypse to reign in the process. Humanity learned to look and look again for hidden barbs before accepting technology's gifts. The most important event in its control was the emergence of the United Nations as a true world government. This began as a purely economic phenomenon as nations joined together in continental trading blocs and the Net dissolved barriers of time and distance. The Global Market became a de facto reality, linking first the markets of the advanced nations and then the entire world. The U.N. Economic Charter formalized the arrangement, spelling out the rules for world trade. The Economic Charter didn't embrace free trade in a real sense. It drew clear distinctions between wealthy (Line One) and poor (Line Two) nations—and it deliberately preserved those distinctions. Nevertheless, it provided a framework that nations could use to resolve differences without force of arms, and provided penalties for those that tried to use force anyway. Third-world countries cried "Imperialism!"—and they were right, but the fact was they were better off within the Economic Charter than outside it. Some sought to bring the system down for reasons of their own, but the advanced world backed the Charter with military power out of pure self-interest. Eventually the advanced nations wound up backing the U.N. itself.

With the specter of war gradually fading, the U.N. turned itself to the other horsemen. The key was population control. Beneath the U.N. banner, world population growth slowed and finally stopped. By 2050, eight and a half billion souls inhabited the planet. The population bomb had been defused—barely—and hunger and disease began to recede as well. The U.N. expropriated and decommercialized the major agribusiness companies, and genetic engineering began to yield results that made sense for the planet instead of the bottom line. Biotechnicians provided designer crops—pest resistant, high yield, and low maintenance—for every ecosystem. Families of crops grown together renewed the soil and prevented erosion while producing complete diets for the masses of the third world. Simple modular systems based on wind and sun brought electricity to the most remote points on the globe. With electricity came sanitation and health care. The Net extended itself until the most primitive village had access to the world's information resources. Most important, the realization came that there were limits, that expansion could not go on forever.

As with the Global Market, these changes were soon formalized, this time in the U.N. Social Charter. The Social Charter guaranteed basic human rights for the entire race. However, the advanced nations declined to back the Social Charter with the military force they applied to the Economic Charter. The Line Two conditions of the Economic Charter were carried over to divide the enforcement of human rights in have and have-not countries. In the have-nots, only the most blatant violations would lead to U.N. intervention. The Line Two countries were not required to implement the full range of the Social Charter's groundbreaking standards for personal welfare, criminal justice, and health care—and few could afford to do so. Everyone's lot improved under U.N. rule, but those who benefited most were those who needed the least to start with. Poverty no longer meant desperation, but neither did it offer hope. The Line Two stipulations ensured the division of wealth would continue as it always had. The situation bred discontent. Bush insurrections began to bubble throughout the third world, disrupting the delicate economic infrastructure the U.N. had built up but never quite becoming large enough to trigger U.N. intervention. Life spans in Line Two countries began to shorten again, but the first world didn't deign to notice. The U.N. had formed UNSEC, the U.N. Space Exploration Corps, and was pouring its resources into unlocking the wealth of the Sol system. In 2042, UNSEC moved an asteroid into Earth's orbit, providing a virtually inexhaustible supply of metal. The profits went to the Line One industries that had paid for the venture. The standard of living in the first world went up again. The standard of living in the third world continued to slide.

In 2055, the discovery of the Tal-Seto stardrive returned hope to the overcrowded masses of the third world. UNSEC added an I for Interstellar to its name and became UNISEC. UNISEC soon discovered two planets that could be made to support life, and undertook an ambitious colonization program. First call on colony slots went to Line One citizens, but there were few takers. By contrast, a groundswell of enthusiasm rose in the third world. A slot on a CT—one of the great Colony Transport ships—meant release from the grinding cycle of poverty and violence that was the lot of most citizens of the poorer world.

The colony vessels were huge, but even so they had room for only a tiny fraction of those who wanted to go. Riots and protests broke out and began to threaten the stability of half the world. The U.N. responded by opening Mars for colonization and commencing the construction of orbital habitats. It built a fleet of CTs and vastly enlarged Earth Transfer Station (ETS), the orbital satellite built originally to service the fledgling lunar colony at Farside. Colonists crammed into shuttles like cattle and boosted to ETS in a never-ending stream. They traveled on the CTs in conditions barely better than those in steerage on a nineteenth-century windjammer. Still the multitudes clamored for colony spaces. The expansion meant almost nothing in terms of the chance of a colony slot for most of those who wanted one, but the symbolic importance far outweighed the reality. It proved the U.N. could respond to more than the basic needs of the Line Two citizens, and in doing so it quelled unrest where armed force had been unable to do so. Technology had finally given the human race a gift without a hook and in doing so it opened the galaxy to the species, but at the same time it unleashed its most dangerous barb yet.

The year 2055 saw the introduction of the Turing Processor Cores—optical computers that used the uncertainty principle to govern their computations. The architecture of the TPC was modeled on the human brain, and it should have come as no surprise when the fifth TPC built became self-aware—and collapsed into recursive self-contemplation, resulting in the collapse of the North American Multi-Modal Traffic Control network. The disaster killed thousands, and the U.N. imposed a state of emergency on the entire continent. North America was paralyzed for a week. Shortly thereafter, other TPCs reached awareness—with results ranging from comical to devastating. No one appreciated the full danger of the situation until a TPC at the University of Chicago established a network link to an experimental manufacturing facility in the engineering building and began to produce mobile subunits to serve as its eyes, ears, and hands. The panicked university administration evacuated the school and called the police, who in turn called in the military. The military tried to establish a cordon sanitaire around the engineering building. The TPC responded by producing subunits with weapons and the situation continued to deteriorate. Eventually, the U.N. authorized the military commander to employ an orbital particle beam, which disarmed and destroyed the TPC but annihilated the entire campus in the process.

In 2060, the U.N. Security Council responded to these events by passing an emergency ban on "life-emulating technology." In 2063, the General Assembly made the ban permanent through Resolution 1212, which went further and put the brakes on a wide range of research. The U.N. Police were given extraordinary powers to suppress any technology that might lead to artificial intelligence (AI). Unlike most U.N. resolutions, this one hit hardest in the Line One nations. Line Two nations were finally in a position to catch up to their wealthy neighbors. The gap between rich and poor began to narrow as researchers in the first world decried Resolution 1212's erosion of Social Charter freedoms. As the U.N. tightened its grip on research, the political battle lines were drawn. In 2082, the Alliance of Free States, a breakaway group consisting of the advanced nations of North America and the Asian Pacific Rim, declared their secession from the U.N. The U.N. responded with force—only to find the Alliance ready. The violence level escalated until a single fusion warhead leveled Atlanta.

Desperate last-minute negotiations staved off a holocaust, but for the first time in seventy years the specter of war had returned. The world was divided and a cold peace developed, a peace continuously broken with "isolated incidents" as both sides frantically rearmed. In the Alliance, AI research resumed in secret, spurred by the demands of the newly resurgent armed forces. Military starships were developed as the strategic importance of Sol-space and the colonies became clear.

In 2111, the tension snapped. Faced with a large and growing gap in combat capabilities brought on by Alliance technological research, the U.N. attacked. The first phase of the war was short and brutal—automated weapons destroyed each other by the thousand. The vast resources of the colony worlds and the asteroid belt poured into cybernetic production facilities, but even the entire industrial might deployed by the two factions proved unequal to the task of replacing the losses. A major battle in the 2120s could eat up 95 percent of the forces involved in less than ten minutes. Sneak raids and lightning probes became the norm.

The war progressed in violent fits and starts, interspersed with periods of almost-peace while the combatants rebuilt their depleted weapon stocks. Life for most people continued as in a city under siege, with day-to-day privations but little actual danger. When attacks broke through the defenses there was massive devastation, but attacks were rare and even the successful ones were over in minutes. Most casualties never knew what killed them. As the years passed, the balance of power shifted inexorably in the U.N.'s favor. Its larger resource base gave it the edge in a war that had become one of high-technology attrition.

In 2134, however, the balance of power reversed itself instantly and irrevocably. Alliance scientists working on man-machine interfaces made a breakthrough that allowed what had never been possible before—human control of the split-second decision loop of automated combat systems. The war was effectively over as soon as it was deployed to the field. It was code named HYPE.

The end of the war saw the dissolution of the U.N. as a formal political organization, but the Alliance Treaty spelled out the same political realities in a document that placed U.N. member states back into their old roles as Line One or Line Two nations. It reinstated and updated the Social Charter in the Alliance nations, but left the disenfranchised citizens of the former U.N. to fend for themselves. Those who could do so emigrated to the Alliance—but for most, the colony worlds remained the most viable option. The third-world exodus continued with renewed fervor and the Alliance encouraged the flood.

For those fortunate enough to live in the Alliance nations, the new Social Charter was an enlightened document, not only in the way it provided for and enforced universal freedom and justice but in the way it dealt with those who violated its tenets. It established Corrective Services, an organization dedicated to the protection of society. C.S. recognized that crime was a dysfunction between individuals and society and strove to bring the two into harmony. The organization devoted itself to removing the criminally insane from the system, treating them, and releasing them if possible. The merely criminal, it put through an extensive and effective program virtually guaranteed to turn them into productive and law-abiding citizens.

The Social Charter carefully spelled out the C.S. mandate and the means the organization could employ. Corrective Services maintained a deep-seated sense of justice and no concept of mercy. It trained its officers to deal with their charges with compassion and understanding, an approach that allowed them to apply the C.S. program without pity or remorse. The program itself sprang from a deep understanding of the forces that drive criminal behavior. Under the Social Charter, justice for a convicted criminal had three goals: punishment, rehabilitation, and restitution. Recognizing the impossibility of performing all three functions at once, Corrective Services applied them sequentially.

Punishment was up to six months under the harsh discipline of a Corrective Services labor camp. The routine was demanding and punitive. Prisoners were deliberately denied sufficient food and sleep. They faced continually increasing demands that spiraled past any prisoner's ability to meet. Under the stress of relentless hard labor, prisoners rapidly reached the point of collapse and were forced beyond it. The treatment was brutal but the time frame was deliberately short, for humanity is endlessly adaptable. That which does not destroy me makes me stronger. In the historic past, the designated enemies of tyrannical states had adjusted to conditions far harsher than those Corrective Services could allow itself to impose. By denying prisoners the time to adapt, Corrective Services maintained its punishment camps as an effective deterrent and ensured that inmates entered the next phase of the program in an eager and pliant frame of mind.

Rehabilitation took place in special rehabilitation centers, self-contained villages whose only walls were the vast distances separating them from civilization. Each one functioned as a working community, a modification of the original tribal group that was the first society. Each member had to earn a place and learn to cooperate for the common good. Rewards and punishments came from a member's peers, not from an external and possibly capricious administration. The communities had to function economically as well, producing enough to pay for food and supplies. In the close-knit atmosphere, the members learned anew the links of interdependence and trust that bind a society together.

There was no set duration for a member's stay in a rehab center. Corrective Services judged each case on its own merits and had no qualms about leaving someone in a rehab center for life. Members earned permission to leave only by demonstrating their ability to function in society. Some stayed on by choice even after they earned release, preferring the intimacy of the village to the faceless anonymity of the megacities where most of the world's population lived. They found themselves roles as mentors, guiding new arrivals through the resocialization process. Corrective Services remained unobtrusively in the background, counseling and evaluating but interfering only in true emergencies. The only direct control it maintained was over the transportation links between the remote centers and the outside world. It was enough.

After the reborn citizen returned to society, the responsibility for restitution remained. Community service programs provided a framework through which society reclaimed its due—time devoted to the communal good. At the same time, it drew its wayward lambs back into the fold. Continual counseling helped to identify developing problems before they became serious enough to land the individual in trouble with the law again. Corrective Services helped to ensure that returned citizens developed a social network through their community service obligations. By giving the individual a valuable, positive role in society, these obligations broke the cycle of crime before it had a chance to become established.

The system was not always fast, but it worked. Corrective Services pointed proudly to its record. Less than one percent of those it returned to society ever committed new offenses. Fewer than one in a thousand were judged incorrigible and sentenced to life in a rehabilitation center. Corrective Services did not give up easily. Before consigning a criminal to this category, it made sure there was no biological imbalance that would respond to drugs nor any emotional problem that would respond to therapy. Incorrigible prisoners were not criminally insane, nor were they socially acceptable. Most of those deemed incorrigible spent their lives in the rehab villages, productive citizens in their microcosms as they could not be in the larger world.

A tiny fraction, less than one in a million, refused to conform even in this environment. They presented a problem, for they could not be allowed to disrupt the delicate community fabric that formed the core of the rehabilitation program. Some persistently escaped, braving hundreds of kilometers of desert or tundra to short-circuit the carefully planned system. There was no easy solution. Corrective Services allowed itself no shortcuts. It could not consign such individuals to a treatment asylum because they were not insane. It could not release them because they were not rehabilitated. The Social Charter specifically outlawed both perpetual punishment and the death penalty, even if the justice-driven C.S. directors were able to countenance such barbarities, which they were not.

But all organizations adapt to the challenges they face, and Corrective Services was no exception. The Social Charter demanded that it treat or rehabilitate all those who had harmed society. It carried out its mandate successfully in all but one in a million cases. And for those who would not or could not conform to the requirements of the program there was Mare Stellatis. Once a lunar observatory, then an Alliance military base, it became a Corrective Services rehabilitation center whose isolation-space was the far side of the moon.

No one who went in ever came out.

CHAPTER ONE

JUDGMENT

"**L**EWIS TYRELL, *being fit to stand trial, you have been found guilty of the following crimes against society.*"

The flight attendant at the front of the shuttle was demonstrating its safety features, miming along as the voice on the intercom described them. Another flight attendant helped Tyrell strap into his seat, pretending to ignore his bright red prisoner's uniform with the black broad arrow on front and back and the handcuffs that held his wrists behind his back. Tyrell was a tall man, with an almost hungry leanness to him. His dark hair was cropped short for ease of maintenance rather than style. His face and complexion were Caucasian, but the tone of his skin and the slight epicanthic fold in his eyelids hinted at Asian genes somewhere far back in his ancestry.

The shackles were tight and Tyrell knew the cuffs would cut painfully under the acceleration of takeoff. His escorts knew it too, but ignored his discomfort. There was hardly any need for escorts; he had nowhere to run on the boost-shuttle. Nonetheless, there were two of them, and they both looked muscular and capable. Doubtless they practiced their unarmed combat daily. At first Tyrell had admired the way the female one filled out her loose-fitting Corrective Services jumpsuit, but her icy gaze had reminded him of the realities of the situation. Since then, he'd kept his eyes to himself. He had no wish to antagonize his captors.

There was a time when the handcuffs would not have been an extraneous precaution. During the war, Tyrell had commanded a Pathfinder platoon, the elite of the elite. But since the peace he had gotten soft, his military service nothing but a memory he would rather forget. In the Pathfinders, he had done at least three grueling hours of physical training every day, unless he was actually on operations in the field. He had deliberately maintained his hand-to-hand skills at a level that would best any of his troops, but that was a long time ago now. In the civilian world, he had neither time nor need to maintain his fighting edge. He was still in good shape, better than average for his thirty-three years, but he was no longer much threat to two Corrective Services escorts.

The attendant moved down the aisle, checking the safety belts of the other passengers.

"Conspiracy to commit a crime . . ."

The assignment was as standard as the Pathfinders ever got. Intelligence sources reported that the Alliance had developed a new drug, code-named Hype. Information was sketchy on exactly what it did, but it was clear that the Alliance thought they had a war-winner. Finance tracers found the initial clue. Over two billion adjusted dollars had funneled through a Singapore-based company called Terradyne. Further investigation led to a secret Terradyne research facility hidden in the Sierra Nevadas, in western North America. The mission was simple. Penetrate the facility, acquire as much information as possible, including above all else a sample of the drug, then destroy the facility and the scientists who ran it and get out.

Planning had taken two solid months. Satellites had been among the war's first casualties, so the operations group had to wait while reconnaissance pilots went in to get imagery. Taking off from bases deep in the South American jungles, they crossed the Pacific coast of North America at just over twice the speed of sound. Threading the valleys and passes at night was dangerous in its own right but it was the only way to penetrate the Alliance regional air defenses. The research center had its own antiaircraft defenses as well, all out of proportion to its size; the importance the Alliance attached to it was clear. Three pilots died before they had the imagery they needed.

Two things were clear immediately. The first was that there was no way an air insertion would work. A fat, slow transport would be easy meat for the missiles, even if the Alliance didn't have a single interceptor on line to scramble. The second was that the platoon would need a lot more intelligence before they could move.

The second problem was easy; Tyrell just bounced it back to Intelligence. If they wanted the drug, they'd have to get him detailed layouts of the base, find out where the inhabitants worked and slept, the guard routines, all the minutiae that went into planning a raid. While Intelligence worked on that, Tyrell trained his soldiers. He had the Engineers build a mockup of the laboratory compound site. As soon as it was far enough along to use, he moved his platoon in. They slept in its guard barracks and ate in its mess hall, and mounted guard duty on the schedules Intelligence provided. He also pulled them out to stage raids on the mockup with another platoon guarding it, after which he gave scathing debriefings designed to drive his troops to ruthless efficiency. He updated the scenarios and the mockup as new data came in. By the time Intelligence was ready, the platoon was ready.

The first problem was also easy to solve, from a Pathfinder's point of view. The installation's isolation was its Achilles heel. It would be very difficult to get to, but there would be no quick rescue when the attack came. They would only have to face the defenses that were there when they arrived. Further, the guards wouldn't be alert. For them, guarding the remote outpost would be a dull but secure job far from the real war. Safe beneath their elaborate air defense umbrella, they wouldn't expect a ground attack to emerge silent and deadly from the dark.

Tyrell's unit would walk in across more than a hundred kilometers of mountain and desert. Everything they needed they would carry on their backs. It would take them three days of forced march to cover the distance. The war had come down, as wars always did, to a handful of soldiers and what they could carry.

"*. . . possession of a restricted weapon . . .*"

The shuttle was taxiing for takeoff, thumping gently as the tires negotiated gaps between the concrete slabs of the apron. The intercom chimed, and a pleasant baritone spoke with a unplaceable accent. "Ladies and gentleman, this is your Captain speaking. Welcome to ASA flight six-sixteen, Osaka to Earth Transfer Station. We'll be taking off on schedule today, and our flight will take about two hours. Local time at our destination is 17:24, Greenwich Mean Time. Once takeoff is complete your cabin attendants will be serving a light snack. Until then, we ask that you leave your seat belts securely fastened."

The intercom chimed again and went silent. The pilot sounded confident and sincerely interested in their well-being, although he must make the same speech three or four times each working day. Tyrell wondered how he did it.

His escorts ignored the announcement; they had clearly been to space before. Once the shuttle started moving they relaxed their vigilance slightly. They felt sure their charge wouldn't escape now. That was the critical moment with sentries. The instant they made the internal decision that there was no immediate danger, they became vulnerable. The man in the window seat was looking out at the airport terminal passing by. The woman in the aisle seat was glancing at some magazines.

For a moment Tyrell considered escape. His martial arts were rusty and hers would be right up to date, but he weighed more than she did and surprise would be on his side. The pair had made a tactical error by not putting her in the window seat. Mass went a long way to offset speed and finesse in a face-to-face brawl in an awkward, confined space. If his hands weren't cuffed he could release his seat belt. When she settled down to read, he could then grab the release on her seat belt, lunge sideways to his right, and knock her into the aisle before she could react. He'd be on top long enough to disable her; he could break her arm if not her neck. Her companion would be hampered trying to undo his own seat belt and his weapon was holstered on his left, against the wall where it would be hard to draw. Tyrell could grab the woman's weapon, doubletap first the man, then her. None of the passengers or cabin crew would interfere with someone so clearly armed and ready to kill. He would move to the cockpit to shoot out the radios and order the shuttle to stop. Back out of the cockpit to yank the lever beside the forward hatchway, blowing the hatch open and activating the emergency slide just as the helpful flight attendant had explained during the safety lecture. Down the slide to commandeer the "Follow Me" vehicle, which would have stopped when the shuttle did. Airport security was tight around the terminals, but the perimeter had nothing but a twelve-foot chain link fence topped with barbed wire. He'd ram one of the fence posts and take the fence down, immobilize or kill the driver, and switch clothes. He'd be free like a running fox.

Except he was handcuffed, and maybe that hadn't been such an unnecessary precaution after all. Surprise and initiative were the key to victory—*Fortune Favors the Bold*. That was what the Pathfinders had given him, and it was something that civilian life couldn't take away. That morning he had clipped a safety pin to the inside of his uniform cuff. It would have served to pick the lock of the shackles and open the door to his escape, except his escorts had taken it away when they'd searched him. Attention to detail—it marked them as professionals. The safety pin was laughable as a weapon, could have been there for any number of reasons, but they'd taken it away just in case. That tiny act had just saved both their lives, and neither one would ever know it.

So many details went into an operation, but you only paid for the ones you forgot. You started with the basics—how to strip and assemble the magrifle, load, unload, and reload it, clear feed jams and cycle jams, set the sights and calibrate the range finder. He didn't need to think about it—his hands remembered for him, as they remembered dozens of other drills for other weapons, other tasks. That kept his mind free for the things he *had* to think about, things like fields of fire, battle formations, point rotation, comm-scodes, morale, fatigue, air support control, and navigation. The list was endless, but a single over-looked item could be disastrous. For a long time after the war, his hands had felt awkward without a weapon in them. Attention to detail had once marked *him* as a professional as well.

". . . forced entry with unlawful intent . . ."

The shuttle swung onto the runway and lined up for the takeoff. The engines spooled up, their whine rising to a throbbing roar that over-whelmed the buzz of conversation in the cabin, reaching a level that was almost painful. The craft shuddered against its brakes for a moment as the pilot stabilized the thrust, then leapt forward. The acceleration forced Tyrell back into his seat and he felt the skin on his face tighten. The handcuffs began to cut into his back as his weight surged to thrice his eighty kilos. The wheels thudded against the runway blocks in an increasing tempo. The craft lifted clear and began climbing steeply. Almost at once the pilot threw them into a sharp bank, held it for a moment, then leveled out heading east. Their ascent steepened, adding gravity to the burden pushing his spine against the cuffs. It felt as though they were going straight up, although in his head Tyrell knew their climb angle was just over sixty-five degrees. Outside the window there was a flash of gray-white as they penetrated the cloud cover, and then they were into clear blue sky. The blue grew noticeably darker as he watched.

He remembered his last takeoff on operations, a much gentler takeoff in a graceful, deadly assault transport that skimmed the waves on ground effect. Then the discomfort had been due to his combat gear, seventy-five kilos of it. The flight to the Pacific coast of North America had taken eight hours, but he remembered only the cramped boredom.

The long patrol in was a blur as well, endless nights marching over rock and sand, always forcing the pace. Daybreak brought fitful slumber beneath draped camfiber, broken by the regular watches they all stood. Everything they brought in they brought out, even urine and feces. They would dump it when they reached a river, not before.

One memory stood out, etched sharply against the grueling boredom of the march. On the second night, a gunship nearly surprised them somewhere in the Tehachapi valley. The rearguard spotted it coming over a ridge and the tiny force had gone to ground beneath the scant cover offered by the desert scrub. It passed directly over them, occulting the moon with its lethal bulk, rotors whispering in the night. The patrol remained frozen in place, lying motionless. Somewhere in the darkness, the gunship would have a partner. They were hunting, searching the desert floor for prey. Tyrell's camfiber combat uniform matched his infrared output to the background by dumping waste heat into chemical chill cans. As long as he lay still he should be invisible, but the system wasn't perfect. There was no way to know if he'd been spotted, if the gunships had circled back and were watching for movement to confirm a target. Seconds dragged past as he lay still and silent. How much time would buy safety? Every minute not moving meant a harder march, forcing the pace even more to reach the daybreak objective.

After an hour, Tyrell gave the signal. In silence his troops shouldered their rucksacks and the little column moved on through the night.

" . . . *and murder.*"

Within minutes, the sky outside the shuttle window went black and Tyrell could see stars past the Corrective Services man's head. The pilot slowly pitched up their flight path until they were truly vertical and the pain in Tyrell's wrists and spine increased accordingly. Abruptly the roar of the engines cut off. It was instantly replaced by a deeper, more powerful note as the boosters ignited. The cabin shook violently and the acceleration slammed them back into their seats. The pain intensified, but Tyrell ignored it. He was no stranger to pain and he had suffered worse. There was a dull throb in his thigh, not quite pain any longer but there whenever he happened to think of it. The throb marked a scar, a deep circle three centimeters across where something, he'd never learned what, had penetrated his quadriceps and lodged in his femur. He hadn't noticed when it hit, although later the pain had been unbearable. Another fraction of an inch and he would have bled to death through a torn femoral artery without even knowing what was happening to him.

The line between life and death was just that narrow. He had a dozen more scars like it, gained on half a dozen missions. The odds were against long-term survival in the Pathfinders. Any of the wounds the scars marked could have been fatal. In any event, none of them had been. Strength and skill only went so far; after that it was up to fate. He had been lucky in a job where few saw their luck hold for long. He'd beaten the clock—come through the war alive and relatively whole. Most of his force hadn't.

The raid was etched in stark detail in Tyrell's memory. The research base was a small fortress, ringed with a triple fence of barbed wire. The gap between the fences was full of mines and the middle fence was electrified. Guard towers reared up every two hundred fifty meters and buried sensor lines reached another hundred meters from the fence line into the surrounding scrub. There was no question of going through the barriers undetected. Instead, they had deliberately triggered the proximity alarm several times on a hundred-meter front where the perimeter sensor strip entered a small depression. They knew from Intelligence that the enemy would send out sentries in a skimjeep. Animals caused false alarms around the perimeter several times a week. The sentries would expect nothing unusual.

The skimjeep had arrived, the sentries alert but not primed for trouble. They checked the area and reported it clear, then died on the points of first section bayonets. The Pathfinders had trained Tyrell to use dozens of different weapons and weapon systems, but he had always favored the bayonet. It never broke down, required no ammunition, and needed no maintenance. And it was silent.

The skimjeep returned with two of first section in place of the sentries. The gate guards opened the barriers as a matter of course, never realizing their mistake. Eight hundred meters beyond the perimeter, a magrifle set to subsonic spat twice. The guards crumpled as the jeep swept past. The remainder of first section sprinted for the gates as the magrifle spat again. The sentries in the towers nearest the gate had no time to raise the alarm.

Second section followed first while third section moved its support weapons out of the underbrush and into positions to cover the raid and the withdrawal. The clock was ticking and they were committed. If the control officer in the guard command post decided to do a communications check with the gate or the watchtowers, they would be caught. It was a calculated gamble.

The alarms were still silent when the skimjeep slid up to the post. Its occupants jumped out, kicked in the door, and killed everyone inside.

They were in.

It took no time to locate the research building; the training mockups had been exact in every detail. By the time Tyrell arrived, the way in was already secure. He led second section through the front doors and down the corridors, guided by first section sentries posted at the intersections. They quickly made their way to the main lab.

The mission was going like clockwork. Their time budget allowed them fifteen minutes to ransack the lab for documents and to find a sample of the mysterious Hype drug. Second section commander divided the room, assigning a search team soldier to each area. They began gathering everything they could lay their hands on. There would be time to sort it later. The demolition team began setting their charges. Tyrell started searching through a series of cryonic coolers where test samples were stored in liquid nitrogen. The first was full of frozen brains, the second contained tissue slices and test tubes. Tyrell checked his watch— ten minutes remaining. He opened a third cooler—empty.

WHAM! A blast shook the building. Tyrell recognized the hypersonic shock of a shoulder-fired kinetic energy missile. It was followed by the crackle of magrifles. First section had bumped something large enough to call for anti-tank rounds. The plan was out the window—they were out of time, but he still hadn't found what he was looking for. Frantically, he continued searching. Nothing in the coolers. He began rifling through a series of cabinets above them. Another blast nearly rocked him off his feet. That was a tank main gun, firing at the building. The tempo of the magrifle fire began to build up, interspersed with the deeper, longer bursts of third section's support weapons. If the enemy had armor, Tyrell's force was in serious trouble. Another WHAM! underscored the point. They had to get out *now* or they wouldn't get out at all. He gave an arm signal to second section leader, who returned a thumbs up and began directing his unit out of the room. Tyrell continued to yank open cabinets.

There! One of the steel doors was locked. He yanked on it but it refused to yield. He stood back and pumped a round from his magrifle into the lock. The mechanism shattered, but when he yanked the handle again the door refused to budge. He cursed and grabbed a detpak from his combat harness, slapped it against the lock, and punched the timer for two seconds. It beeped its warning as he dived for cover behind a heavy workbench. The blast showered him with broken glass, but when he ducked back around, the cabinet door leaned crazily open.

Inside was a foam nest with niches for a dozen vials. They were shattered, spilling a clear viscous fluid. If there was more time he could have salvaged some. He cursed and turned to leave. The last of second section was already gone.

Something caught the corner of his eye. An intact vial! The glass was thick, and the vial had been sealed by melting the open end shut. It was labeled in neat handwriting—HYPE 1131. He grabbed it. No time to unseal the padded and cooled container built specially for the mission. He just stuffed the vial into the inside breast pocket of his combat tunic. There would be time to look after it when they made it out of the base compound. He didn't allow himself to guess the odds against that occurring.

Second section leader was waiting outside the lab door; the rest of the section had already gone ahead. Tyrell gave him a thumbs up and they ran down the corridor, the trooper covering left, Tyrell automatically watching right. There was no rank in situations like that, you just did what you knew needed to be done.

The firefight had died away when they got to the exit. That could be good news or bad. There was blast damage and a burning fighting vehicle in the courtyard, but no time to evaluate the situation. Second section should be securing their retreat from the next fallback point. If it wasn't, they would find out soon enough.

A cannon burst took his section leader as they rounded the corner of the building. Instinctively Tyrell threw himself sideways and down. He rolled to his feet and found himself looking down the barrels of half a dozen Alliance magrifles. Behind them two main battle tanks and a platoon of combat skimmers covered the central compound. Bodies where strewn across the concrete like rag dolls.

One of the Alliance troops barked a command. Slowly Tyrell put down his magrifle and stood up, hands spread out above his head. It was then that he noticed the blood gushing from his thigh. Strangely, there didn't seem to be any pain. A lance of fire stabbed from the hillside beyond the main gate, the firing signature of a KEM. Across the valley a gunship exploded into flames. A second later the WHAM! of the launch and the dull *whoomp* of the explosion hit them. Another gunship pumped cannon fire back at the hillside. The *crackcrackcrack* of a magrifle on automatic answered from the darkness. Whatever was left of third section was conducting a fighting retreat.

His vision settled on one of the bodies. It was Valdi, section leader Valdi, first section commander. The left side of her combat uniform was a bloody pulp. The right side was torn away, revealing the delicate curve of her breast. Her eyes were closed, as if she were merely asleep. He remembered her as a vivacious young woman and a tough, competent soldier, always cool under fire and a crack shot. Now she looked so terribly young and vulnerable, weighed down by the remorselessly utilitarian gear she carried.

He was a good commander and he knew his troops, but when he tried to remember something else about her nothing came to mind but the fact that she was twenty-six. Of the rest of his command he could remember nothing at all.

"In consideration of these crimes you are sentenced to one day of punitive confinement . . ."

The roar of the shuttle's engines cut off, and they were falling free. For a single panicked second Tyrell thought something had gone disastrously wrong, that they were going to take the long drop from the edge of space, but his escorts seemed unconcerned. He had never been to orbit before, but for them the sudden weightlessness was clearly routine. The flight attendant was coming down the aisle checking the passengers for motion sickness, one hand on the guiderail on the cabin roof. His escorts relaxed completely, there was nowhere he could go now. They would fall all the way around the planet until their orbital loop caught up with ETS. There Tyrell would be transferred to a cargo pod and put aboard the Moon Shuttle for delivery to his ultimate destination.

He remembered falling when the pain hit. His leg was torn and bleeding and wouldn't hold his weight. He didn't even remember injuring it. The Alliance soldiers had encouraged him to his feet with the butts of their weapons. When he'd collapsed again they kicked him until he crawled in the direction they wanted. When that was too slow, they dragged him, beating him all the way. A sudden explosion brought a grim smile to his lips. The charges his team left in the research lab had gone off. He'd scored a victory they couldn't take away, although they made him pay for it with their boots. He'd spent the night locked in a storage shed converted to a makeshift guardhouse along with a handful of survivors from his platoon. All were badly wounded. Groggy as he was, it made him proud. None of his soldiers had surrendered while they could still fight. They did what they could for the wounded, then fell into exhausted sleep. Twice during the night, they were awakened as bleeding members of third section were thrown in with them. By daybreak there were fourteen of them. By noon two had died. There was no food or water that day, and that evening they were beaten again, systematically and in turn, and so far as

Tyrell could see, to no purpose. They didn't even ask him any questions.

That evening he'd been taken by the SIS, the dreaded Security Intelligence Service. They flew him out in a bounce jet, where to he didn't know. They had questions for him, many, many questions. He knew how to resist interrogation, how to spin out tiny fragments of information for hours. He made them work for it, but ultimately he knew they'd win. It was their game and he knew they'd break him with drugs if they even suspected he was managing to hold out on them. Command never gave operational troops anything but mission-critical information for exactly that reason. He gave them everything they asked for, eventually, but they never asked him about the vial he took and so he never told them.

". . . one thousand days restitutive service . . ."

As long as he had the vial, he could still complete his mission. He guarded it as though it were life itself, sneaking it through strip searches and snap inspections in his tiny cell. When the SIS were through with him, they would send him to a prison camp. His leg would heal and he could escape from there and somehow make it to Mex-

ico. Mexico was part of the Alliance—enemy ter-
ritory—but a lot of U.N. sympathizers lived in the
back-country. If he could reach them, he could
reach the U.N. If he could complete his mission,
the sacrifice of his unit would not have been in
vain. The vial became his reason for living. It gave
him a focus that helped him hold onto his sanity
through the grueling interrogations.

Eventually he'd wound up in Camp 14, an
ugly barbed-wire scar on the beautiful Bullion
mountains. He immediately began planning his
escape. The obstacles were formidable. There
were over two hundred kilometers of mountain
and desert before the Mexican border. That didn't
matter; the mission was no longer for U.N. Intelligence but for personal redemption. He could not
allow his troops' deaths to be in vain. He had to
purge his soul of their blood, whatever the cost.

It took him three months to prepare, most of
it spent on self-administered physiotherapy for his
wounded leg. He had escape rations, a survival
kit, a water container, maps, and an address in
Quetzal that could lead him to the Mexican
underground. He knew as much as the prison
camp intelligence system could learn about
Alliance internal security measures and check-
points. The risk was high, but he was undaunted.
He would return the precious vial to U.N. Intelli-

gence or die trying. Only one event could stand between him and his redemption.

The end of the war.

". . . and rehabilitation at Mare Stellatis."

When the Alliance and the U.N. signed the treaty, he was already over the wire and running hard through the Algodone dunes, closing on the Mexican border. He didn't even know the war was over until he picked up a week-old newspaper page blowing along an empty desert highway, with *VICTORY!* in a banner headline across the front. It was an Alliance victory, of course. The news hit him like a kick in the stomach. Had the U.N. won, he would have been debriefed, given his report, and been officially demobilized. He could have handed over his prize and put some sort of end to his quest. As it was, he simply stopped running because no one was hunting him anymore. There was no point in trying to report—the dismantling of the U.N. meant there was no one to report to. Instead, he made his way to Los Angeles. It was as good as anywhere else—since his father had died he had no place to call home. No one tried to stop him; he was just another displaced refugee. When he got there, he applied for Alliance citizenship.

Much to his surprise, it was granted, perhaps because he was already there. Something in him needed to be close to the mountains that bore witness to his failure. Perhaps he thought they could give him atonement.

Five years later, there was a reunion of sorts. All twelve survivors of Fourth Platoon Pathfinders came. It was the first time he'd seen any of them since the SIS took him away for interrogation. It was an emotional event for them all as they recalled their triumphs and defeats. At the end of the evening, they drank a toast to their fallen comrades and Tyrell showed them the vial. It was the first time he'd looked at it in years, it was a half-forgotten trinket that spent most of its time buried in the bottom of a box of not-needed-now-but-too-important-to-junk junk. Now it was important as a symbol. It was his way of telling his troops that they had not failed. Their final mission had been a success, no matter how the war had ended. He wanted to wash away their guilt, to take it upon himself and thereby cleanse them all of their collective failure. It made a difference, he could see it in their eyes. That night he slept the sleep of the innocent for the first time since the end of the war.

The next day the SIS kicked in his door, seized the vial, and arrested him. They bundled him into an airvan where a gray, expressionless man read out the charges against him. The words were a blur but certain details stood out. Conspiracy, robbery, assault, murder. He protested his innocence to stony, expressionless faces.

The charges were real, but they didn't belong to him. When they arrived at the holding center they put him in an isolation cell, normally reserved for the most dangerous offenders. The gray man smiled without humor and left as the heavy cell door slid shut. Tyrell collapsed on the narrow bunk in anger and despair.

It had to be the Hype—that was the only possibility. They hadn't interrogated him, they had only taken the vial. No one had known he had it. The SIS must have figured his mission for a failure and at the end of the war he was just another displaced person in a world full of refugees. No one had known of the vial and its secret until he'd revealed it at the reunion, and the next day the SIS had come. Whatever Hype was, someone with reach and power wanted to ensure that its secret remained hidden. Someone who had gained influence over one of his soldiers. Not even the SIS could simply disappear a citizen, the Social Charter saw to that. But they could drop him into a ready-made criminal trial and make sure that he and any knowledge he might possess stayed safely in the Rehab system for a long, long time.

And then he had broken down and cried. It was not the prospect of a Corrective Services punitive labor camp that tore the sobs from his body; he had endured worse and could do it again. It was the knowledge that one of his own had betrayed him.

The next day his trial was held behind closed doors. His C.S.-appointed defender sat in stony silence while the evidence was read in and the witnesses called. Sealed monitors recorded the event, for under the Social Charter justice must be done and seen to be done, even in closed trials. But the defender never called Tyrell to the stand, and so he never said a word in his own defense.

But he had laughed when the judge pronounced sentence. Not even the SIS could make citizens disappear with impunity, but no one ever came back from Mare Stellatis.

CHAPTER TWO

IMMOLATION

THE MOOD CHANGED as the shuttle approached Earth Transfer Station. ETS grew from a point of light until it filled the forward windows, spinning slowly as it floated against a backdrop of brilliant stars. The psychological wall between Tyrell and his escorts dissolved a little as they shared the majesty of the scene. ETS was a huge cylinder, spun around its long axis to provide artificial gravity. It was immense and still growing, one of the first pieces of infrastructure to be restored after the war. The shuttle pilot lined up on the axial docking bay and began a slow roll to match their rotation with the station. As their spin increased, the station seemed to slow and stop, while the Earth, the moon, and the starscape began to revolve around them in stately silence.

Two starships floated serenely beside ETS, attended by a host of smaller craft. They were immense in their own right, too large to dock with the station, but nonetheless dwarfed by its bulk.

They were matched with it in orbit but revolved along with the rest of the universe as the shuttle spun on its long axis.

The larger ship was a Highliner CT, one of the fat colony transports, laden with supplies for some new outpost of humanity circling some distant star. Its passenger spaces would be jammed solid with colonists, mostly from overcrowded Line Two nations that could afford to implement the Social Charter in name only. The chance to carve out a living on an untamed world was an opportunity that came to only a select few. On its return voyage the vast ship would carry colony grown grain for the Line Two masses, a cargo made economical only because the CT would have to return empty otherwise. The Highliner was rotating on its own, more quickly than ETS, and as it turned its name came into view. CTS *Hope*.

Behind the transport was the distinctive silhouette of the AC *Lexington*, half shadowed by the station's bulk, like a predator crouching in the darkness to wait for prey. The *Lexington* was an Alliance light cruiser that had fought hard in the war. Now her mission was deep space exploration. The conversion of the powerful and deadly cruisers to peaceful purposes was highly publicized, but Tyrell could see her weapons suite was complete. Insurance against the unknowns on the edge of explored space and, perhaps, insurance against another breakdown in the global power structure.

The station grew larger until it swallowed the shuttle. The little craft nestled into a shiplock within the docking bay, settling under perhaps a fiftieth of a G. The massive shiplock doors ground shut behind it and air flooded in. Once the pressure stabilized, the docking arm swung across and the entryway opened. Tyrell felt the wall between himself and his captors go up again. The magic moment was over.

Most of the passengers were lining up to collect their baggage and clear transit protocols for their final destinations. Tyrell's escorts flashed their C.S. badges and took him past the formalities to an anonymous office with windows looking down on the passenger arcade. It was bustling with people of every description. Young and old, rich and poor rubbed shoulders as they bustled from arrival to departure, united only in their desire to be somewhere else. A solid mass of humanity jammed a cordoned-off strip that ran nearly the whole length of the arcade—colonists waiting to get aboard *Hope*, each clutching the few kilograms of personal possessions that would be their only link with Earth for the rest of their lives.

There was a brief conversation between his escorts and the ETS Security duty officer. When it was over, his escorts handed over the keys to Tyrell's handcuffs. Significantly, they didn't hand over any paperwork. He was now officially a non-person. When he disappeared into Mare Stellatis, there would be no way to trace him. His escorts left and the security officer locked him in. It would be another three hours before the lunar shuttle was ready to launch. In the meantime, there was no need for anyone to waste time watching him.

There was an opportunity there. ETS Security officers weren't of the same caliber as the Corrective Services pair. The room he was locked in was an ordinary office, with a desk and a bookshelf. There was a ventilation grille overhead. Under the tenth G the station's rotation provided at this level he could easily jump up and grab it, then wriggle through the ventilation system and escape. As soon as he was sure he wouldn't be interrupted, he began rifling through the desk drawers for something to pick the handcuffs with. It was difficult work because he had to do it with his hands behind his back, looking backward over his shoulder and keeping an ear open for a key in the lock.

The second drawer yielded a paper clip. Painstakingly he restored the drawers to their original condition, or as close as he could get them. Then, sitting down and facing the door, he began to carefully probe the lock on his cuffs. It wasn't the simple spring release he'd hoped for, but he kept working on it. While he worked, he planned his escape. Getting out of the office was only the first, easiest step. Once the cuffs were off, he would crawl into the ventilation system. Assuming he didn't get stuck or blocked somewhere, he would find some place to leave it in reasonable privacy. His first choice was an unoccupied private living compartment where he could find some clothing. Anything, no matter how ill-fitting, would be better than the bright red, broad arrow he was now wearing. Anonymous clothes would prevent his immediate recapture.

After that the problem grew more complex. Certainly the alarm would be raised very quickly. Getting off ETS would require stealth and planning. Ships were leaving all the time. If he could figure out how to get on one, he could pick and choose his destination. Getting through security was the catch. Even without an escape alarm in force, it would be difficult—if not impossible. He lacked a ticket, a passport, even basic identification. Without them, he was a sitting duck. Stealing someone's wallet might get him enough to get through a cursory check on the passenger arcade, but there would be a retina scan prior to boarding and there was no way he could fake that. Even if he somehow got past it, by force, wit, or bribery, there would be another check at his destination, and no way to prepare a way to dodge it.

Behind his back one of the locking pins clicked into place. He had a good mental image of the lock's mechanism now. There were three pins. The paper clip was a poor tool for manipulating them, but with patience he could do it. Then a small twist and it would pop open. ETS Security would be in for a surprise when they came to get him.

As if inspired by his success with the lock the solution to his larger problem came to him. CTS *Hope*, the colony ship. If he could get to her, he would simply blend in with the anonymous mass of colonists. There would be no identity checking at their destination, whichever distant and unciv-ilized world it was. The colony would be glad to have another pair of hands. He could start anew and leave behind SIS and the ghosts of his war as well. Getting access to *Hope* wouldn't even be as hard as getting on a commercial hop. Unable to dock, the CTs were serviced by localhaulers, light reaction vehicles used to transfer cargo and pas-senger pods. Force, wit, and bribery *would* get him on one of those, and with no documentation requirements there would be no problem. Perhaps it would be as simple as joining the jammed lineup in the arcade below. Getting a colony slot required documentation, he knew, but that was mostly to impose some order on the process of filling boost shuttles on third-world runways. Anyone in that lineup on ETS would be assumed to have a colony slot, because no third worlder without one would have got onto the station otherwise, and any first worlder who wanted to go could get a slot for the asking.

A second pin clicked into place behind his back. Now that he had a broad plan, he began to fill in the details. There were two courses open. He could either break out and try to get aboard the CT as soon as he escaped or lie up for a few days to let the alarm die down before making his move. The first option was attractive, as it left him exposed for the minimum amount of time. The problem was that he had to be on board *Hope* before Security discovered his absence. If the hue and cry went up while he was in the middle of the attempt, he'd be caught for sure. The second option meant he'd have to hide through the entire search, perhaps for days. That was a risk, but if he went immediately into hiding and didn't try to make it to the CT he'd be more likely to evade the searchers. Of course, *Hope* might depart in the meantime—but there would be another Highliner along before that happened. The CTs ran like a high-pressure pipeline, trying frantically to deliver colonists desperate for space to colonies desperate for labor.

On balance he favored the second plan. Getting aboard a Highliner was a problem that would require some study. Taking the patient approach would give him the time he needed. He'd only have one chance to get it right.

He stopped thinking about it, concentrating his attention on the shackle lock. Delicately he manipulated the final pin, being careful to not dislodge the first two in the process.

The door slid open, revealing two men in ETS Security uniform. Without changing his expression, Tyrell palmed the paper clip behind his back. He applied pressure with his wrists to torque the lock mechanism and prevent the two pins he'd picked from popping back into place. It was early for the lunar shuttle. Perhaps the guards were merely checking on him.

The weren't. They grabbed him by the arms and unceremoniously hauled him to his feet. The tension came off his wrists and he felt the tiny *click* of the pins falling back to the locked position. All his painstaking progress had been wasted. At least they hadn't noticed the paper clip. ETS Security wasn't half as professional as Corrective Services had been.

They led him down to the passenger arcade.

Travelers turned to stare as he passed, horror and fascination mingled in their faces. Their reaction underscored his outcast status. The guards and handcuffs marked him as an unperson, an object to be examined and talked about rather than a fellow human being. From the passenger arcade he was taken through a series of corridors to a cargo bay full of shipping containers. They led him to one that stood open, waiting. Loaders working in the bay stopped to watch as the guards tossed him in.

The container was full of thermoplastic crates of various sizes, strapped against the walls and floor. No attempt had been made to adapt the container for a passenger. There was no heat, no light, no ventilation. The guards closed the doors, and there were clacking noises as they sealed them shut. Tyrell was left in total darkness. Resignedly he began working on his shackles with the stolen paper clip. At least when he arrived at Mare Stellatis he wouldn't be helpless in the face of whatever dangers it presented. Several times his progress was stymied as the container was subjected to sudden acceleration. Clanks and scrapes told him he was being loaded aboard the lunar shuttle. Finally, he gave up until the disturbances ceased, then patiently began again.

Eventually he got the handcuffs off, and then there was nothing to do but wait. Without a watch, he quickly lost track of time. He dozed fitfully. The temperature rose and fell, varying from uncomfortably hot to freezing. Occasional periods of gentle acceleration broke the monotony; otherwise there was only dark silence. His greatest fear was that the container would be somehow delayed or misshipped and his air supply would expire before he arrived.

When he was awake he wondered about his destination. When he was asleep he dreamed of it. He had heard of Mare Stellatis—Sea of Stars—of course, everyone had. And he knew exactly as much as anyone did. It was as far away from a lunar sea as you could get on the lunar surface. Originally it was an observatory, built on the far side of the moon to shield it from Earth's light. It was named for the breathtaking view from its instrument dome.

During the war, Mare Stellatis became a support base for the far-ranging Alliance starships. Robot mining machines tunneled far beneath it into ice-rich mineral seams. The water they yielded was shipped to Farside Colony and refined to provide reaction mass and deuterium to power the warships' fusion power plants.

The end of the war saw the abandonment of Mare Stellatis. The astronomers moved to observation platforms in deep space; the starships found their ice in Saturn's rings. The installation lay frozen and empty until Corrective Services found a need for it. Rehab candidates whose case files were tagged INCORRIGIBLE were sent there. Like all rehab centers, Mare Stellatis was a functioning socioeconomic microcosm earning its keep in the larger world. Its economics were brutally simple. The rehab candidates mined water, which was shipped to Farside Colony. The colony extracted the deuterium for power and sold the water to commercial users, mostly for reaction mass. A percentage of the power went back to the prison for life support. No water meant no power. The inmates of Mare Stellatis had to produce or suffocate in freezing darkness. Unlike other rehab centers, however, there were no counselors, no C.S. staff to provide guidance. People Corrective Services sent to Mare Stellatis were, by definition, unrehabilitatable. There was therefore no point in trying.

No one knew any more than this, but speculation ran rampant. There was no communication whatsoever between the rehab center and the outside world, lest some determined escaper should arrange for outside help—surely the only means of escape through the barren vacuum of the lunar surface. Some thought Mare Stellatis was a living hell where violent anarchy was barely counterbalanced by the need to meet the relentless ice quotas. Others thought the place was an official lie, a Corrective Services bogeyman designed to motivate its charges to modify their behavior, or a cover-up for a secret execution program that weeded the incorrigibles out of society. More outlandish theories existed, complete with extensive and bizarre research to back them up. Sometimes when news was slow, the netfeeds and newstapes would trot out the weirder theories and popularize them for awhile.

The real truth was, no one knew.

The shuttle grounded with a gentle *thump*. Tyrell knew they were down because of the gravity. The moon's pull was no stronger than the shuttle's acceleration, but it was constant and unvarying. It couldn't be long now. Despite the frightening unknowns looming in front of him he was relieved—the air was growing stale. Whatever the horrors of Mare Stellatis, they couldn't be worse than slow suffocation.

After a time, there was a series of jolts and some swaying, followed by a sudden, howling rush that could only be an airlock cycling. Not knowing what to expect, Tyrell waited in nervous anticipation. For a long time there was only silence, and his imagination began to fill in the emptiness with nightmare scenarios. *I must not fear*, he told himself. Fear paralyzed the will. *I must not fear*. He crossed his legs in lotus position, closed his eyes, and breathed deeply. It was a technique he'd learned long ago from his first martial arts instructor. His mind conjured up Beethoven's Ninth symphony. He had not practiced the technique in years, not since the war. As he lost himself in the music, the fear and fatigue washed away. *I should have done this before*, he thought to himself, and wondered why he hadn't. It was the last thing he thought of before his consciousness was fully submerged in the flow of the symphony, and he became without self.

His mind had gone so far away that at first he didn't notice the tools banging on the container seals. Then the doors opened and a painful flood of light poured through the opening. Ears popping with the sudden pressure change, Tyrell fell from nirvana with a jolt. He sprang into a fighting position, a relaxed stance that supported attack or defense but did not seem too aggressive. He balanced on the balls of his feet, gauging the gravity. The glare was a major handicap, but he would have to accept it. Shielding his eyes with his arm Tyrell squinted past the glare, discerning a handful of figures.

"Well, well, a newling." A man's voice, deep and neutral, offering neither threat nor welcome.

"Ooooh, can we eat him, hmmmm?" A woman's voice with danger in it. She purred like a cat contemplating a goldfish.

"Quiet, Storna." Another voice. A figure advanced out of the glare into the darker interior of the container. "Welcome to hell, newling. What's your name?" The speaker was a slight, bookish man, dressed in loose-fitting pants and shirt belted at the waist, and carrying a pad on a clipboard.

"Lewis Tyrell," he replied and thought *I can take him, if I have to. Can I take them all?* He shifted his position ever so slightly, defense taking priority over attack.

"I'm Stelchek. I see you got your cuffs off, saves us having to cut them." The stranger offered his hand and Tyrell took it cautiously, keeping his guard. Stelchek noticed his reticence. "Don't worry about Storna, we don't bite." He looked around the container. "Are there any more with you?"

"No."

"Come with me, then." Stelchek took him by the arm and guided him out of the container. The remainder began organizing the unloading of the supplies. There were seven in the group, four men and three women. Storna was a tall, buxom negress who moved like a cat. She licked her lips provocatively at Tyrell as she passed. Her challenge was unmistakable. The others watched him with varying degrees of curiosity and indifference.

Once outside, he blinked and looked around. He was in a brightly lit airlock leading to a largely empty loading bay. A series of openings in the far wall led to corridors beyond.

"This lot can handle the unloading," Stelchek told him. "Come with me and I'll show you around." He raised his voice, directing it to the group in the container. "I'm taking the newling down to Vincennes. Stack and rack; I'll verify everything later."

"Sure, Checker, it's done." The speaker was a tall, lean woman with Asian features and long, dark hair.

"Thanks, cheri." Stelchek waved and led Tyrell through the bay and into one of the connecting corridors.

The corridor was warm, clean, and brightly lit. The air smelled pleasant, reminding him of redwood trees. The only noise was a gentle but omnipresent susurration of moving air. Tyrell walked as if in a dream. He had been ready to fight for his place in a society of violence. He didn't know how to react to the reality. He responded automatically to Stelchek's small talk, but his mind was trying to resolve the incongruity.

The corridor curved gently to the right, broken every hundred meters by T-junctions where other tunnels led away, also to the right. Stelchek led him to the first junction. The cross tunnel ran straight, intersected by more tunnels every fifty meters.

"The City is laid out in concentric circles," explained his escort. "Armed forces dug 'em when they expanded the base. The axis tunnels meet under the observatory dome." Stelchek was still nattering on.

"City?" asked Tyrell, coming out of his reverie.

"That's what we call it, the City and the Garden—that's Upside. I suppose it's really more of a town." The short man cocked his head, thinking for a moment. "There are around two thousand of us."

"Is there a Downside as well?"

"There is. Vincennes will tell you about it."

Before Tyrell could reply, voices rose around a corner, followed by a group of two women and a man.

"Got a newling, Checker?" The taller, dark-haired woman called as they came into sight.

Stelchek led Tyrell up to the trio. "Newer than morning snow," he confirmed, then gestured formally. "This is Lewis Tyrell. Lewis, this is Cynthia." He indicated the woman who had spoken. "Miklos and Michelle."

"Mike and Miche." The two names sounded almost alike, and the man put his arm around the blond woman to indicate they were a pair. He put out his hand. Tyrell shook it.

"Pleased to meet you," Miche smiled, too invitingly for half a couple.

He smiled back, not saying anything. *I don't know their social codes*, he thought.

"Catch you at Social, Checker?" asked Cynthia, looking at Tyrell.

"I'll be there."

The group moved off, leaving Tyrell feeling somewhat off balance. Stelchek noticed his expression.

"You look surprised."

Tyrell shook his head. "I can't believe this is the dreaded prison of the damned."

"Not what you expected, is it?"

"I didn't really know what to expect, but not this."

"Vincennes will explain everything to you. It's not far."

They made their way down the radial corridor. Tyrell counted a dozen intersecting ring corridors. Stelchek greeted other groups of three or four as they passed, pausing to exchange a few words and introduce Tyrell. He seemed to know everyone. The atmosphere was relaxed and friendly, but Tyrell noticed that people deferred ever so slightly to his companion. After a while he asked about it.

"I'm The Checker," his companion answered, as if it were a complete explanation. Tyrell could hear the capital letters.

"I thought that was your nickname."

Stelchek smiled. "No, it's my job description. I'm The Coordinator's right hand. I check things."

The Coordinator, thought Tyrell. More capital letters. "Like what?" he asked.

"What we have in storage, how much water we're shipping to Farside, what we need to order from C.S. and how much water it's going to cost us, who's not showing up for roster work, that kind of thing."

"And Vincennes is the coordinator." Tyrell made it a statement rather than a question.

"Yes. He sets things up, I make sure they happen, that's the way it works. We're not much on formality here, but there has to be *some* organization."

The brightly lit corridor ended in a circular chamber with seven other entrances. They were obviously in the city's central hub. Bulletin boards lined the walls, covered with a hodgepodge of hand-drawn posters and notices. What looked to be the work roster Checker had mentioned occupied a large board all by itself. A ramp spiraled up and down in the center of the room. Checker gestured and Tyrell went up the ramp, the shorter man following him. *Can I trust him at my back?* Tyrell wondered, unconsciously raising his alertness level to a potential threat. Mare Stellatis *seemed* benign, but he couldn't shake the preconceptions he'd come with even in the face of the reality. The ramp led into a round chamber the same size as the one below, but without the corridor entrances. Instead, there was a desk surface running around its outside edge. Scars on the surface and against the wall marked the spots where equipment had once been mounted. Portable wall units sectioned off part of the room. The ramp continued up another level.

Checker pointed to the divider. "That's the Coordinator's office. This used to be the observatory instrument room. Above is the dome. Just wait here a moment. It's a public area, but Vincennes likes to work up there. I'll just see if he's free." Checker continued up the ramp. Left to his own devices, Tyrell looked around the room. There wasn't much to see. Clearly all the scientific equipment had long since been removed. The room's only adornment was the continuous work surface. With nothing else to occupy his attention, he examined the walls. They were covered with some kind of sprayed foam insulation beneath a resilient skin. Tyrell pressed against the material with his fingertips. The material was spongy beneath the tough covering. *Is it pressure tight?* he wondered. There were shinier patches in places, showing where rips had been repaired. *The repair materials must be supplied from outside*, he thought. *How much contact do they have with the outer world?*

"Vincennes will see you now." Checker waved a hand at the ramp. Wordlessly, Tyrell mounted it, the smaller man again following.

The dome was done up as a formal garden, with ferns and potted plants arranged artistically around walkways. It was beautiful—but the thing that caught and held his eye when he reached the top was the view. It was spectacular, and it drew his eye to the zenith almost against his will. The instrument dome was a thin shell of long-chain polycarbonate, a perfect hemisphere a hundred meters in diameter and so transparent as to be invisible. The setting sun was impaled on a jagged spire on the crater rim, like an impossible diamond scepter. Overhead, the Milky Way spilled across the infinite black canopy as fifty thousand discernible stars burned down with undiminished intensity. Earth's familiar constellations were nearly lost in the riotous beauty. Tyrell felt almost drunk at the sight. With only the delicate one-sixth G holding him down, he felt as if he could dive straight up into the limitless sea of stars.

"Mare Stellatis. Beautiful, isn't it?"

Reluctantly, Tyrell tore his gaze away from the splendor. The speaker turned out to be a middle-aged man, balding but powerful looking. He had a wicked scar across his left cheek that stood out starkly against his dark complexion.

Stelchek made the introductions. "Lewis Tyrell, Anton Vincennes, our Coordinator."

"Thank you, Checker, you can go now." Vincennes's voice was quiet and calm, but his aura of command was unmistakable. *A natural leader*, thought Tyrell. He consciously relaxed against the instinct to respond to the man's authority.

Stelchek nodded and went back the way he'd come. Vincennes remained silent until the smaller man was gone, then spoke.

"Welcome to Mare Stellatis, Lewis Tyrell." His voice was somehow distant, and he didn't offer his hand. Unsure of how to respond, Tyrell remained silent.

Vincennes waited, watching. Tyrell consciously relaxed himself, refusing to let himself be made uncomfortable. After a few moments the other man spoke again. "There are only a few rules here." He held up a finger. "First, when there's work, everyone works. Checker will show you the schedule board."

Tyrell nodded.

"Second." Another finger. "Don't make waves. You have a problem, settle it sensibly. If you can't settle it, bring it to Checker or me."

Tyrell nodded again.

"Third, don't try to escape. See those blocks?" He pointed and Tyrell followed his gaze. Twenty-centimeter cubes ringed the base of the dome. "C.S. has the basin under surveillance. If they catch anyone outside, they'll detonate those and pop the dome. They took all the pressure seals out when they converted the base. If they do that we're all dead. Understood?"

"Understood." *Corrective Services has been clever*, he thought. *Escape for one means death for all. In a prison of hard-core escapers, social controls function where physical barriers fail.*

Vincennes lowered his fingers and offered his hand. His scar wrinkled as his face relaxed into a smile. "Welcome to hell."

Tyrell accepted the handshake, relaxing as well. "I have to say it doesn't seem much like hell to me."

"Not what you saw on the newstapes, is it?" Vincennes seemed amused.

"No."

The Coordinator gestured to a sort of padded couch, set low on the floor beneath a miniature palm tree. *What do they do with the plants during lunar night?* Tyrell wondered. The padding looked too thin for comfort, but under one-sixth G it turned out to be luxurious. When Tyrell was seated the Coordinator moved an amorphous cushion over and reclined on it. Once he was settled, Vincennes continued. "Let me ask you this. What were you expecting?"

"Anarchy, violence." Tyrell shrugged. "Forced labor to meet the ice quotas. I really didn't know what to expect."

"But not this?"

"No."

"Nobody does. Too many vids about the horrors of Mare Stellatis. There's drama in making it hellish, and the government is happy to let people think that's the way it is. But think about how Corrective Services works. Are you criminally insane?"

"No."

"Of course not, or you wouldn't be punished, you'd be in treatment on Earth. Are you stupid?"

Tyrell remained silent. *What is he driving at?*

Vincennes considered him for a moment, then spoke. "I'll take that for a 'No' as well. It wouldn't matter if you were. The Rehab programs don't require intelligent candidates to be successful."

Tyrell made a cynical gesture. "They wouldn't be successful if they required intelligence."

Vincennes smiled. "Exactly. Corrective Services turns criminals into upstanding citizens. Even the dullest thug can be salvaged. Almost every criminal eventually learns to conform and contribute to society. How, you ask?" He paused before answering himself. "Classic conditioning, punishment and reward. A monkey would respond to it, or a dog."

"So? This is common knowledge."

Vincennes spread his arms. "So ask yourself— who would fail to respond? Only those who find the need to *not* be conditioned outweighs the punishment-reward system. Those who don't want the trinkets society offers in return for toeing the societal line. Those who choose to decide on their own what's right and wrong. Free thinkers. The incorrigibles." He laughed. "Us."

"And this is your society, this . . ." Tyrell groped for a word.

"Paradise?" Vincennes filled it in for him.

"Is it paradise?"

"It is for our kind of people. Life is beautiful, as you'll learn. We eat well—Checker will show you the Garden later. Most of the population is young and vibrant. All of it is intelligent and independently minded. That's what it takes to get here. C.S.

straightens out the misfits and malcontents down on earth. They never make it up here. We have a rich social fabric, what more could you ask for?"

"And the work?"

"We share the work, but it's not onerous. Right now, the roster portions out fourteen hours per week per citizen. That's deskwork or light labor and doesn't include kitchen shifts. More demanding jobs have a time bonus, if you'd rather get more time for yourself."

"What about the ice mines?"

"We don't mine ice."

"But . . ."

"We don't mine ice." Vincennes was emphatic. "The Downsiders mine ice."

More capitals, thought Tyrell. *Language cues. Things of importance have special emphasis.* "The Downsiders?" he asked.

"You think you've hit rock bottom, consigned to the oblivion of Mare Stellatis. You haven't. We have a good life here. Pull your weight and follow the rules and you will too. Cross us—" the Coordinator's face hardened. "Cross *me*, and you go down the mine. If you want violence and anarchy, that's where you'll find it."

"A prison within a prison." Something was tugging at Lewis's awareness.

"Exactly."

"For freethinkers? Incorrigibles?" *Test him, see how he reacts.*

"Don't play games with me, Lewis Tyrell—you'll lose." There was a certainty in the man's voice that went beyond menace.

"Well, I'll be careful, then." With another part of his mind Tyrell wondered, *Why am I pushing him like this?*

"We'll see." Vincennes's manner was formal. *Have I made an enemy of this man?* "You'll find Checker waiting downstairs to get you settled." The Coordinator's manner had stiffened. *If so, I have been foolish.* Vincennes turned around and looked up at the starscape, deliberately putting an end to the conversation. After a few moments, Tyrell turned and left. Something was still tugging at his attention, but he couldn't quite put his finger on it.

Stelchek was waiting for him at the base of the stairs. He greeted Tyrell with an open hand. "How was your chat?"

Lewis shrugged. "It left me with more questions than it answered."

"Vincennes can do that to you. That's why I'm here."

"He mentioned a garden. I'd like to see it."

"Of course. Why don't we get you some decent clothing first. You won't want to wear the red arrow."

"How is that arranged?"

Stelchek grinned broadly. "I'm the Checker, I set you up. You get some advances when you arrive. You'll have a few more roster hours at first, to make up for it."

The short man led him through a radial tunnel opposite the one he'd come in through, down a ring tunnel and into a large room. In the room, two men and a woman were making cloth on a hand loom two meters across. They worked with practiced skill, the woman working the levers while the men tossed the shuttle back and forth between them and applied the beat rod. Another woman was working a pedal-driven spinning wheel. Black stone pots of dye, sewing paraphernalia, and miscellaneous tools cluttered workbenches. Bolts of fabric filled shelves around the walls. The rustic feel of the scene was marred by the occasional modern tool, including a pair of robotic flexstations configured to cut and stitch cloth. Spools of spun yarn caught Lewis's eye. Most of them looked handmade, but some were clearly synthetic fiber wound by machine. *They stretch the resources C.S. gives them. How far, I wonder?*

The woman looked up from her spinning. She was attractive, middle-aged, although lunar gravity made her figure look younger. "What's up, Checker?" Her penetrating glance at Tyrell showed the question was rhetorical. Stelchek answered anyway. "Got a newling, Lewis Tyrell."

"Pleased to meet you, Lewis. I'm Lorili, Lori for short." She stopped pumping her wheel and put her work down. "I guess you'll be wanting some clothes."

Lewis smiled back at her. "Please."

She got up and went over to a series of large bins against one wall, beckoning Lewis to follow. The bins were full of jumbled clothing. "I can give you three shirts, two pairs of pants, and a pair of moccasins." For the first time, Tyrell noticed the handmade footwear everyone was wearing. "Plus I can trade you for what you've got on." She looked him over. "Say a sweater?" The question was half directed at herself, half at Checker. He gave a tiny nod in acknowledgment. Tyrell noted the gesture. *She could have made that decision herself. Checker has power here.*

"Help yourself." Lori gestured to the bins. Lewis rummaged through them. The group at the loom stopped their work and came over to watch as he tried on his selections. Finally he wound up wearing dark blue fatigue pants and a long-sleeved smockshirt in heavy black cotton belted at the waist, and ankle-high moccasins. His other selections were piled on a worktable beside the bins—two more smockshirts, another pair of fatigue pants, and a synthfiber sweater.

Checker rested his hand idly on the pile. "How many workhours there, Lori?"

She ran a practiced eye over the garments. "Say ten for a newling. Put on another ten and I'll round up his perspace stuff." She noticed Tyrell's questioning expression and added "Sheets, blankets, stuff like that. No aesthetic choice involved."

Tyrell nodded. Checker made a note on his pad. "Seems fair. OK, Lewis, they're yours. Hold the rest for him, will you, Lori, until we find him somewhere to stay."

"Sure, Checker. Nice meeting you, Lewis." She sat down by her spinning wheel again as the weavers went back to their loom.

"What's perspace?" Tyrell asked as they went out.

Checker laughed. "Local dialect. Personal space, where you're going to live. You can choose just about anything. Mare Stellatis held two hundred thousand during the war, plus fleet crew and transients. We aren't short on room. But we'll see the Garden first."

The short man led Tyrell back down the way

they had come, then up to another ring tunnel. He felt disoriented by the encounter with Lorili and the weavers. They seemed too *soft* to be part of Mare Stellatis. And Stelchek. He clearly held authority, but not through force or personality. Only Storna's aggressive greeting and Vincennes's unsettling warning fit his preconceptions. *Like jujitsu*, he thought. *Where you expect resistance, there is none.*

"How do you organize things here?" he asked Checker.

"Well, there's the Coordinator and the Checker, as I told you. That's me and Vincennes. We have about fifty work groups with different jobs, and each group has a leader who represents them on the Council. How the team is set up internally is up to the team itself. The Council breaks down what needs to be done and the teams take care of it. Everyone does basic roster work and kitchen duty; everyone eats and breathes and gets the basics. If you want more than that, it's barter trade with whoever has what you want, or extra work hours for community services."

"What about disputes?"

Stelchek shook his head. "Not generally a problem. There's more than enough for everyone here. I have a dozen monitors—semiformal police, but they don't have too much to do. We don't get many malcontents—I'm sure Vincennes explained that to you?" He waited for Tyrell's nod. "Those we get, go Downside."

Further conversation was cut short as they came to a hole in the floor, four meters in diameter, fenced off with a guardrail and with a pole running through it, like the pole in a firehouse. Without hesitation Checker jumped, grabbed the pole and slid down. Tyrell went to follow him, but—unlike a firepole—this one went down and down beyond the vanishing point. *Is this a test?* he wondered. Checker was already fifty meters below him. *Fear paralyzes the will.* He jumped and grabbed for the pole.

The ride was exhilarating. The low lunar gravity enabled him to control his speed with just a light touch on the pole. The sides of the vertical shaft blurred past and he laughed aloud as he fell. Landings flashed by at regular intervals, but when he looked down, Checker was still falling below him. He released the pole and let gravity accelerate him until he overtook the other man, then had to grab on hard to keep from colliding with him. The friction of the pole burned his hands, but he didn't notice.

Suddenly heat and light blazed and Tyrell was, momentarily blinded. When his vision returned he saw he was suspended in a vast cavern. Above him, ranked suntubes shone down with warm brilliance. Far below him was a patchwork of green and blue.

The Garden rose up to greet them, and they landed in a grassy meadow, the pole rising up from it like a fairy tale beanstalk. Tyrell looked around, inhaling the rich, organic scents. It smelled so *alive*. The cavern was a natural bubble, shaped like a flattened teardrop. Scale was impossible to judge, but it had to be at least a kilometer high and several times that across. Hundred-meter cedars with impossibly thin trunks spread a canopy over lush tuftgrass interspersed with wildflowers. A long beach bordered a lake filled with oversized lily pads. A waterfall cascaded into the lake from an opening a fifth of the way up the wall. Halfway down the lakeshore, a group of men and women were diving from a cliff. When they hit the water it fountained up almost to the clifftop before falling back with unnatural slowness. As they drew closer to the scene, Tyrell could see the bathers were nude. Those not diving were basking on rocks, tangled in casual intimacy. *Relaxed social/sexual boundaries*, he thought, recalling Michelle's too-inviting smile. A gentle breeze caressed his face, and the air was warm and moist.

Tyrell gestured around at the huge cavern.

"This looks volcanic. I didn't think there was any geologic activity on the moon."

"I don't know about the rest of the moon, but there is here, or there was. A big comet hit here, a billion years ago or so. That's where all the water came from. Most of the center of the crater was molten at one point. This is a steam bubble, but there are actual lava tubes as well. That's why they chose this spot for Mare Stellatis, and for Farside Colony, too—it's in the same formation."

"And you've made it into your own ecosystem. Incredible."

Checker nodded and pointed up at the suntubes. "Ninety percent of our energy input goes here." He stooped to pick a wildflower. "These are our lungs. The plants absorb the carbon dioxide and replenish the oxygen. The air picks up heat and moisture here, then rises to carry it up to the rest of the city through the ventshafts." He pointed to the hole they'd fallen through, and Tyrell could make out other openings in the ceiling amid the glare of the suntubes. Checker continued, "As it circulates, it cools and starts to drop. Eventually the moisture condenses out and the cooled air and water comes back to us through the Watercave." He indicated the waterfall's source.

"Convection heating and ventilation."

"Exactly, except on a grand scale. The Garden provides us with everything we need. Most of the work we do involves tending it. We grow all our own food, of course."

"Do you have meat?"

"There's trout and perch in the lake. We have rabbits, chinchillas, songbirds, chickens, even some deer and sheep, although we save those for special occasions. Then there are mice. They're not supposed to be here but they always have been—early stowaways. They make a good stew if you can catch enough of them. And we have cats, which we keep in the City to catch any mice that find their way up. We don't eat the cats, of course."

"Of course."

"Tonight there'll be venison. It's a special occasion."

"What is it?"

"The arrival of a newling." Checker smacked his lips. "There'll be a special social tonight to welcome you."

"Is it that rare of an event?"

"Rare enough to be an excuse for a party. Most of us have been here since the beginning, when Corrective Services cleaned the incorrigibles out of the rehab colonies at the end of the war. Less than one criminal in a million arrives here. We get perhaps a dozen in a year. Population growth isn't a problem."

"You have both sexes here—what about children?"

"We were all sterilized before we came, just like you. Our oh-so-moral government doesn't want to have children born into hell." There was an edge of bitterness in Stelchek's voice.

Tyrell studied the short man for a long moment. *Should I tell him?* "I wasn't sterilized."

Checker looked up at him, waiting for the answer without asking the question.

"They were in too much of a hurry to see me disappear to worry about the fine details." It was Tyrell's turn to be bitter.

The other man nodded. "You're a special transport case."

"A what?"

"Special transport. In the war it was the label they put on prisoners they never wanted to see again. You've never been to a C.S. labor camp, have you?"

Tyrell shook his head. "No."

"Never escaped from a rehab center?"

"No."

"You aren't an incorrigible, you're an embarrassment. Someone high up wanted you out of the way for good."

"So I've learned."

"Why?" The question was flat.

Tyrell shrugged and spread his palms. "I don't know. They've made a mistake."

Stelchek laughed sardonically. "A real innocent."

"No, not an innocent." Tyrell shook his head, thinking back. "Just not guilty."

Stelchek looked at him for a long moment, then looked away. "Let me show you the waterfall."

They took a path to the top of the falls. It led them out of the meadow that the beanstalk pole landed in and through a forest of fragrant pine trees, then out of it again and along its border past cultivated fields where some type of grain ripened in the artificial sunlight. When it reached the edge of the cavern floor, it started up, growing rockier as it got higher until finally they reached a ledge that took them to the cavern at the top of the falls. "This is the Watercave," said Stelchek. Tyrell looked into a huge round cave, the mouth of a natural lava tube. It was unlit, but enough light streamed in from the suntubes overhead to fill the opening with plant life. A steady and rather cold breeze blew from the depths of the cavern and a stream reached back into the darkness to feed the waterfall that spilled over its lip.

After a pause to let Lewis drink it all in, Stelchek spoke again. "This is the other half of the convection cycle. Warm air from Upside cools and filters through Downside until it comes out here, bringing the Downsider water quota with it."

Tyrell dipped a hand in the stream and found it was barely above the freezing point. It swept over the edge of the Watercave and fell away, seeming almost lethargic under lunar gravity. At that point, the stream was divided by a large outcrop. Half of it fell through a series of pools that cascaded down the side of the wall.

"Make no mistake, Downside is cold." Stelchek pointed to the pools. The ones at the bottom were steaming. "Those are all heated. The ones at the bottom are about as hot as you'd want to swim in. That's how we regulate the lake temperature. Come on down and see."

The remainder of the water streamed away from the outcropping and dropped in a series of icy curtains until it joined the last pool, raising a veil of mist where the two temperatures mingled. Vines and creepers spilled down the sides of the falls as if they were in motion themselves. Stelchek led Lewis down an improbably steep switchbacked trail beside the falls. Halfway down, they found a naked couple bathing in one of the smaller middle pools, screened by the mist and their own intimacy.

Tyrell tried not to stare at the woman as Checker led him past. Lunar gravity let her ample breasts stand as they never could have on Earth.

At the base of the falls, Stelchek pointed out a pipe half a meter across that jutted from the shore and dove below the surface of the lake. Its other end was buried in the rocks at the base of the falls "That's how we pay for all this." He swept an arm, taking in the Garden and by extension all of Mare Stellatis. "It leads to the deuterium refinery at Farside Colony. If we don't keep that pipe full we start losing power."

"How much do they take?"

"A thousand metric tons a day. That's what the Downsider quota is."

"Is there ever a risk they won't fill it? They have leverage if they choose to use it."

"We have more than two years of water reserve in the lake. Downsiders like to eat." A grim smile flashed across Stelchek's face. *There is a hidden message here. We have more than leverage, we have power.* Tyrell remembered the Coordinator's warning. Life could be good in Mare Stellatis, if you toed the line. *Why do they need such stringent controls?* That was the critical question.

Stelchek went on, having paused a moment to let the point sink in. His voice was affable. "Let me show you the orchards."

The orchards were an eclectic mixture of citrus trees, vines, and tropical fruits. They reminded Tyrell that he hadn't eaten since he left Earth and he picked a grapefruit. It was fat and heavy, ripe and surprisingly sweet and the juices ran down his chin as he devoured it. If his eagerness and lack of restraint cost him status with Checker, the other man didn't show it. He idly pointed out a small herd of deer, wandering aimlessly and eating windfall. *No, windfall is the wrong word*, he thought. With no wind and little gravity it was a wonder the fruit fell at all. Tyrell noticed the lack of apples. *No seasons, maximum nutrient conversion*. Mare Stellatis's crops were strictly defined by its artificial climate.

Night was a relative term, of course. Lunar night wouldn't arrive for another thirty-six hours—and outside the instrument dome Mare Stellatis lacked even that metronome. The interior lighting ran on a twenty-four-hour cycle. The Garden's management program made a gesture toward morning and evening by varying the intensity of the suntubes across the ceiling. Before Checker finished his impromptu tour, in what might have been midafternoon, people began arriving, dropping out of the sky on the beanstalk-pole. They congregated around a bowl-shaped meadow where a group was building a bonfire. To Tyrell the fire seemed a dangerous luxury in Mare Stellatis's closed environment, but nobody seemed concerned. Stelchek explained it to him when he asked. "Actually, it's essential for balancing carbon dioxide. Right now the levels are low—so we have bonfires at social until they get back up to where they should be. If it goes too high, we start taking dead organic matter out of the system before it decomposes."

The Checker introduced Tyrell to everyone as they arrived. He recognized Miche and Mike, Cynthia, and the Asian woman from the airlock—whose name turned out to be Valia—but beyond that he was quickly overwhelmed by the array of new names and faces. All told, perhaps a thousand people came.

It was strange to see darkness descending while the shadows barely shifted. As the light faded and the bonfire died down to a steady blaze, the group that had been tending it brought a series of whole deer, already dressed and spitted. Huge iron pots full of wild rice were put on to boil. The deer were stuffed with fresh-baked bread and vegetables and roasted over the coals. Fresh fish were wrapped in cabbage leaves and baked in the ashes. Bottles of homemade wine were passed around, robust but dry and satisfying. Soon the inviting odors of cooking food filled the air and Tyrell realized he was ravenous. The group who'd been in charge of cooking handed out glassy black plates and mugs made from fused lunar rock, and set out the food on long trestle tables that looked too flimsy to support the weight of the platters and tureens. A line formed and Tyrell filed past with the others, ladling heaps of steaming food onto his plate. He sat down on a grassy tuft with Checker and began to eat. Mike and Miche came to sit and make dinner conversation, but Tyrell's interest was in the food.

The fish was amazingly good; it had the clean, delicate taste that only fresh-caught trout have. The venison was unlike anything he had tasted before, rich and filling. The vegetables cooked with it had absorbed its flavor and added their own unique notes to the blend. They were unusually spiced but once his palate adjusted to the flavor he found them excellent. The wild rice was served with a thick, savory mushroom gravy and would have made a meal all on its own. Desert was a crisp, fresh fruit salad served in a coconut cup.

Throughout the meal, people continued to come up to Lewis to introduce themselves and welcome him. He responded as best he could, becoming more sociable once the initial edge was off his hunger. Cynthia came and sat beside him, intimately close. At first he was not entirely comfortable with her familiarity but her relaxed, casual manner was disarming and he ended the meal leaning back against her as she idly massaged his shoulders. Her hands were surprisingly strong and agile, and she smelled fresh and female.

He let himself relax, feeling her breasts soft against his back as she soothed his muscles. *I was so tense*, he thought, *I didn't even realize it*. She worked her way steadily down his back, around his ribs and then back up his chest. Somewhere along the line music started from some hidden source. By then he had surrendered himself to her completely. Eventually she kissed him.

It was night by then, or the Mare Stellatis equivalent, and the darkness gave them privacy. By the dying embers of the bonfire, Lewis could make out other couples and groups in various stages of loveplay. Cynthia was unhurried in her attentions, exploring his body with casual affection. *How long has it been since I've been with a woman?* He couldn't remember. She was here, now, and that was all that mattered. They made love and there was nothing in the world but the taste of her skin and her gentle cries. Afterward they lay together, eyes closed and breathing softly, and fell asleep in each other's arms.

Later he was awakened by a kiss. At first he

thought it was Cynthia, but then he felt her lying still beside him. The woman atop him now was more aggressive than Cynthia had been, her kisses demanding a response. The situation made him uncomfortable and he tried to discourage the newcomer without waking Cynthia, but she would not desist. Their movements disturbed Cynthia and Lewis tensed, expecting a scene, but all she did was raise her head and kiss first him and then the other woman. Both times she took her time and made a thorough job of it. Then she settled back down to sleep. Lewis gave up resisting and allowed himself to respond as the woman mounted him. Afterward she lay beside him opposite Cynthia and they slept in a tangle of intimacy.

When the suntubes started to glow on the designated eastern edge of the Garden, Lewis awoke and found himself between Cynthia and Michelle. Mike was curled up behind Cynthia, although Lewis didn't remember his arrival. They were all beneath a colorful cotton blanket that had appeared sometime during the night. As he stirred, Cynthia rolled over and kissed him, affectionately rather than passionately, and got up. Other figures were moving in the growing light. Cynthia went to join them, then came back with breakfast, a platter of leftover rice and venison. Mike and Miche were stirring also, and together they ate the cold provender. They were completely unconcerned with their nudity and made no move to get dressed. *Relaxed social/sexual boundaries*. Lewis compromised by crawling into the loose trousers he'd gotten from Lorili.

After breakfast, they went swimming in the lake and he had to take off his trousers again. The water was brisk and refreshing. He looked around for Checker but the short man seemed to have disappeared. Mike and Miche swam for a while, then went off on their own so he splashed and played with Cynthia, then somehow wound up with Valia. He looked around and saw Cynthia with a tall, dark man with long curly hair. He turned back to Valia, who kissed him and pressed her firm breasts against him. Her nipples were erect, whether from the cool water or sexual excitement he couldn't tell. After a while he didn't care.

Checker found them sunning themselves on the bluff overlooking the lake.

"Enjoying yourself, Lewis?"

Tyrell ran his hand down Valia's back to the swell of her buttocks. Half asleep, she purred in response. "I've decided I might like life in hell after all."

"Today we have to find you some perspace and today your work roster starts. You're on general labor."

He sat up. "Does that mean anything?"

"You just provide help to one of the specialist teams. Everyone starts out like that. If you find you have an aptitude for something, you can change later."

"When do I start?"

"Right now." Stelchek turned away. Lewis kissed Valia on the shoulder blade. She purred again and he drank in her exquisite form, then reluctantly followed Checker.

The way back up from the Garden was the opposite of the way he'd come down. A long cable with loops for hands and feet ran down one ventshaft and up another one, hanging free in a long loop inside the Garden cavern. It moved at a brisk walking pace. Checker grabbed on and was hauled up, swaying gently. Tyrell took a loop twenty meters behind him. Sudden vertigo seized him as the cable pulled him higher. His grip on the cable tightened in near panic. *Fear paralyzes the will*, he told himself. Deep breathing restored his equilibrium. The trick was to keep looking up. By the time they reached the roof of the Garden cavern he was enjoying himself immensely and his sense of equilibrium had returned well enough for him to look down and enjoy the view. The suntubes grew warm, then hot, and then he was in the ventshaft. A few minutes later he saw Stelchek deftly grab a handhold and swing himself onto a landing. He followed less gracefully.

From there they went along a ring tunnel to a section of narrower corridors with doorways leading from them. Each doorway opened onto an empty room perhaps five meters by five meters. A few of the doorways had wooden doors on them to replace the airseals Corrective Services had removed when they rebuilt Mare Stellatis as a rehab colony. Clearly they were for privacy only; they would never hold pressure as the originals had. Checker gestured down the corridor. "Perspace. This is where most of general labor lives. You can move later if you like, but this will be most convenient for now. Take your pick, you can have as much as you want."

"This one's fine." Tyrell indicated the closest opening. The room behind it looked like all the others they'd passed

"Good enough." Checker produced a piece of red chalk and scribed a symbol on the floor by the entrance to Lewis's selection. "I'll have Lori bring your clothes here and arrange for the rest of your stuff. It'll be here when you get back."

They went back down to the tunnel hub

beneath the instrument dome. Checker explained the work roster he'd seen before. Lewis's name already appeared on the list. General labor was a catch-all group and its members were parceled out to assist with more specialized jobs. He noticed that Valia was the group's Council member.

"You're slated to work on the pumps to start, but you'll probably fill in on other things from time to time," Checker said on the way back to the beanstalk pole. They slid back down to the Garden. There he left Tyrell in the care of Tombuol from the hardware group, a large, quiet man with an easy smile. Tombuol showed him the pump room, hidden beneath the rocks of the waterfall. The pumps shipped water through the pipeline he'd seen before to Farside Colony. The machinery was simple and robust and needed little supervision beyond cleaning the screens that kept weeds and mud from clogging the pipes.

It took them two hours to finish the job. It was muddy and wet work, but not particularly arduous. At the end of it, he rode the skycable back up to the city and after a few wrong turns found his perspace. As Checker had promised, his clothing was waiting for him, along with a straw-filled mattress, sheets and blankets, and some boxes filled with utensils and sundries. He was just changing when Cynthia arrived with a vase of cut flowers. "Housewarming," she smiled, then helped him arrange the room's meager contents. When they were done she pulled him down on the mattress. He didn't resist. Afterward, she made it clear she would stay if he wanted her to. *Do I want this?* he asked himself, idly caressing her back. She was lying face down, sated and content, her long dark hair tousled on his mattress. *I need this*, he thought, which didn't quite answer the question. It was enough for the moment. He leaned over and kissed the back of her neck.

The pump station became his regular work site. Every other day he helped clean the screens. On the alternative days he watched as Tombuol taught him how to maintain the machinery. The most important pieces of equipment were the pipeline flow gauge and the lake volume reader. They were the heart of the Mare Stellatis economy. The lake level had to be kept constant by varying the pump rate. The pump rate in turn dictated how much power Mare Stellatis could receive. Any surplus could be used to purchase spares and supplies, delivered in containers like the one Tyrell had arrived in. Every day, Checker showed up to take readings so he could balance the water budget.

The exchange with Farside was only half the economic equation. The other half was Downside, where the ice miners worked. Their food supply was rationed according to the pump rate. One day, Tyrell volunteered to go along with a porter group carrying the daily ration dump to Downside. He was motivated more by curiosity than anything, although the extra work-hour was credited to his account.

He watched as Checker supervised the loading of the food packages to be sent down. The amount of food was strictly related to the amount of water that came into the reservoir lake through the waterfall. There were a few tools as well, pickaxes, tritium lights, sundry hardware, and bales of hay gathered from the Garden. Every item was checked and inventoried before the porters moved off, accompanied by Checker and three of his monitors wearing black armbands. All the porters were balancing improbably large loads and their burdens dictated that they take the spiral ramp beneath the instrument dome rather than the beanstalk pole or the tow cable.

At the bottom of the City, they moved to one of the return ventshafts. The downdraft was cool and the shaft was grated over with heavy bars. The bars had the dull sheen of Arika alloy. *Starship hull metal*, thought Tyrell. *How many cubic meters of water did the Downsiders pay for their own prison bars?* The mood was tense. One of Checker's monitors unbolted a hatch set in the middle of the grate while two more drew stunrods and stood guard. *So Corrective Services will import weapons—at least these*, he thought. He hadn't known that the monitors were armed before. It seemed out of keeping with the relaxed atmosphere of the rest of Mare Stellatis. He found the entire situation disturbing. *And that shows how much this place is changing me*, he thought. Once upon a time he would have felt right at home with the hidden tensions and the potential for violence. Once upon a time, he would have felt uncomfortable without them.

Below the open hatchway there was only darkness. They lowered the packages down on twenty-meter ropes. Movement and voices rose from beneath them and Tyrell could see the greenish gleam of tritium lights. The rope slackened and tightened as the Downsiders untied the packages. Finally the monitors pulled it back up. The hatch clanged shut and the monitors refastened the bolts. It was Tyrell's last job of the day. From there he went to the Garden—he had a date to swim with Cynthia. He soon forgot his disquiet splashing with her in the hot pools beneath the waterfall. They made love in the water and then held each other and he felt at peace with himself again, but afterward the unease returned.

"Are you happy here?" he asked her that evening.

"Happy? Of course, why wouldn't I be?" She said it matter-of-factly as she cut vegetables for stew. They'd decided to eat together in her per-space rather than in the Garden.

"I mean you don't find it confining here? You don't miss the real world?"

She looked at him for a long moment. "In the real world I was a misfit. I couldn't toe the line. I was nineteen the first time I went through Corrective Services."

"What for?"

She put down the vegetables and perched on the counter. "I was on my own in Toronto after my parents died, renting a basement in Rosedale and going to engineering school. I had no money, just a pension from the government because I was seventeen when they died, but I lucked into this place—Rosedale is a very expensive suburb. My pension covered the rent but no food so I went to school all day and worked evenings. It wasn't easy but I was proud of making it on my own. Then I'd come home and my neighbors treated me like dirt, just because I had no money. It didn't matter how smart I was, how hard I worked, what my potential was. All they cared about was the clothes I wore and the place I lived in. Arrogant bastards."

"Resenting snobs doesn't sound like a crime to me."

"I used to run through the golf course there, for exercise. Of course I had to sneak around the fence to do it—not enough money to be a *member*. They didn't want the greens cluttered up with jogging proletarians. There were all these houses backed onto the golf course, big expensive houses. Well, one day I got sick of it. I picked one—a plastic surgeon's, I think—and waited. They went out and I went in, picked the lock and shut down the alarm." She grinned. "You can learn a lot at engineering school if you pay attention outside of class. I put the strip on the place and taped enough in jewelry to feed me for ten years. I mean it. In downtown Toronto you had people literally starving in the streets, let alone what goes down in the Line Two countries. And these guys cruise by in their egomobiles and dump ten years of food on pretty rocks to impress their friends with. It made me sick."

"So what did you do?"

"I kept doing it, of course. I did some research and got the equipment I needed to do it right. It was fun, exciting, profitable. What more could I ask from a career? It beat the hell out of answering phones on the night shift, that's for sure. I was *proud* to put the strip on them, drop a little reality into their shrink-wrapped lives. I got good at it, really good. I dropped half what I made on the aid shelters downtown, just like Robin Hood, you know?"

"And you got caught."

"I did *not* get caught. I was good, I told you that. My fence got caught and turned me in to cut his sentence. I batted my eyes at the judge and got off light, six weeks punishment camp, rehab, and a year community service. Not bad for the cash figures I'd processed. I didn't much care until I hit the labor camp and then I just went insane. I mean, they were *punishing* me. I don't say what I was doing was right, but what those rich guys were doing was dead wrong. It just wasn't illegal—why should it be? They're the ones who make the rules of the game. I wasn't about to do penance for putting the strip on *them*."

"So what happened?"

"I escaped, of course. You'd have to be stupid to remain in that environment voluntarily. They caught me and put me back. I broke out again. It was personal. I could have handled it if I wanted to. The point was, I didn't want to—and they couldn't make me. After my fourth breakout they sent me here."

"Don't you want to escape from here?"

"I came in the airlock ready to break out if I had to breathe vacuum to do it. Not anymore. This isn't a punishment camp, it isn't even a rehab center. It's a wholly separate universe and I fit in here like I never did on Earth. Everyone works, everyone plays. People judge you on who you are, not what you own. They couldn't drag me back now." She laughed. "As if they'd ever try. I'm too dangerous for the real world."

"You're just dangerous enough for me," he said, and kissed the nape of her neck. She melted back into his arms. Later she asked him idly. "What about you?"

"Hmmmm?" He opened his eyes and found hers a few centimeters away. They were deep and blue.

"What brought you here?" Her eyes showed concern.

"A mistake."

"It's more than that." She wouldn't be put off by glib answers, so he told her the story.

"What did you leave behind?" She studied his eyes and he looked away. *She senses my doubt, she knows something is missing here.*

After a time he answered. "Nothing," he said, and he realized it was true. *If she can be content here, why can't I be?* He had no answer, and in her embrace he soon forgot the question.

❖ ❖ ❖

His life fell into a comfortable rhythm over the next weeks. In the morning he slid down the beanstalk pole to find breakfast already prepared by whoever was on kitchen duty in the meadow-bowl. Then he went off to the pump station with Tombuol. After that he would swim to clean up, then bask beneath the suntubes. He avoided the beach where most of the community went to swim, preferring a private spot he'd found where two large rocks formed a tiny inlet near the pump station. Around midday he would go for lunch. Each meal was available for four hours to avoid having to feed the whole community at once. About half the inhabitants came to meals at the meadow-bowl regularly, the other half eating in their rooms or at their jobs. Everyone rotated through kitchen duty on top of the normal work schedule. Tyrell didn't mind the extra work and often stayed around afterward to help out and socialize even when he wasn't scheduled. In the afternoon, he would go for a run around the perimeter of the Garden, starting and ending at the trail up to the waterfall. After that he would swim again, or watch one of the plays or poetry readings put on by various groups throughout the day. At first he was simply a spectator, but as he grew increasingly comfortable with his situation he found himself joining in more and more often.

He spent his nights with Cynthia, sometimes sharing a bed with Mike and Miche or another couple, more often by themselves. For the first couple of weeks Checker and Vincennes had come around to ask how he was doing, but as they saw him settling in, their visits became less frequent. The fifth week saw another feast and Tyrell found himself shaking hands with a disoriented newcomer. In the seventh week, Tombuol taught him how to play chess and they spent hours after work with the game.

As time passed, he felt himself becoming a new person. His old life seemed almost to belong to someone else. And yet sometimes the unease returned, not quite the same feeling he had felt at the entrance to Downside but related to it. At those times he would go exploring—the City was immense and hardly any of it was used. He found little of interest in the abandoned sections, but scouting through them satisfied a need that he was hard put to define. At other times he would go up to the instrument dome and gaze up at the limitless starscape for hours. Cynthia withdrew slightly during those periods, sensing his need to be alone with himself.

Once she asked him. "Why do you go off like that? There's nothing out there but empty corridors."

"I'm not looking for anything in particular."

"Then why go?"

To answer the call, he thought, which didn't make sense even to him. What call? A driving need to conquer the challenges of vacant tunnels? "I don't know." he told her. "I just have to do it sometimes."

If she was unsatisfied with the answer, she didn't show it. There was enough of the young, rebellious Robin Hood left in her to understand his feelings, if not share them. The next day she met him at the base of the beanstalk pole and took him to the waterfall with a picnic lunch. He protested that he had to work but she'd already made arrangements with Tombuol. It was an idyllic day. They swam in the tiny inlet and when they made love she did it with more than her usual boldness and lack of inhibition. She was determined to make him *hers*, to prove she was worth more than an empty corridor. He let her think she succeeded, but the question echoed in his own mind. *Why?*

One day he found the answer, not in a dusty corridor but waiting in Vincennes's office beneath the instrument dome. A pump had begun to leak. Soon it would need a new sealing ring. Tombuol had sent Lewis to find Checker and get an order placed for the next supply shipment. Rather than try to chase Checker down he'd gone to the Coordinator's office, knowing the little man would come by there sooner or later.

He had never had occasion to go there before. Vincennes was out when he arrived, but the door was half open so Tyrell let himself in to wait. The first thing to catch his eye was a map of the base, projected into three dimensions from a ten-centimeter mapcube into a two-meter floating display. A convenient key translated the color-coded tunnel sections. The upper living levels of the City were laid out in neat green concentric circles, ten levels deep. Woven into the pattern were blue lines—accommodations and support facilities for two hundred thousand personnel. Red and yellow marked power and communications conduits, snaking throughout the complex. Blue and white marked water and air routes. But as large as the city sections were, they were only the tip of the Mare Stellatis iceberg. Most of the map was filled with the tangled black skeins of ice-ore tunnels, broken at intervals by orange maintenance stations. Tyrell traced the lines with his finger, thinking. The map answered questions and in doing so raised more.

"You look impressed." Vincennes had come up behind him.

"I had no idea the base was so large."

"There's over a thousand kilometers of tunnels here." The Coordinator seemed to take pride in the fact, as though he had built Mare Stellatis himself.

"What are these?" Tyrell indicated orange blocks on the surface around the crater rim to lunar west. *Be casual. Don't arouse suspicions.*

"Just more maintenance stations, far as I know. Garages for surface vehicles at the tunnel-heads."

Tyrell suppressed a thrill of hope. *Surface vehicles! Don't betray interest.* Aloud, he said, "I don't see the ventshafts."

"This is an old map. See how the Garden cavern is solid blue?" Vincennes pointed. "It used to be a holding tank for the water before it was shipped to Farside. They mined cubic kilometers of it. You can still see the spoil mounds from the instrument dome." He pointed to a thin blue line leading from the cavern to the edge of the mapcube. "That's the pipeline that runs into the lake now. C.S. put in the Garden and the ventshafts when they set up the convection airsystem. Mare Stellatis used to have a ducted system, but convection is lower maintenance and the Garden was necessary for food anyway. All these—" his finger traced the power and air conduits that laced through the projection. "They don't exist any more."

Tyrell pointed to the tangled ice-ore tunnels. "These must all be sealed off, then."

"No, they're open, but they aren't in the con-vection system either. No power, no heat, no light. You go down there and you'll freeze, maybe in minutes, maybe in days, but you will freeze." There was a warning in the Coordinator's voice, a warning deeper than the ice-ore tunnels.

Tyrell answered, carefully casual. "They're all Downside anyway; I don't have to worry about it."

Vincennes looked at him sharply but Tyrell kept his expression neutral. After a second he said, "What can I do for you, Lewis?"

"I'm waiting for Checker, but maybe you can help me," he replied, glad to have moved to a safer topic. He outlined the situation with the leaking pump. Vincennes agreed to make sure spare pump seals were included in the next supply order. The Coordinator showed no more suspicions and Tyrell gave him no more reason to harbor them, but when he left he was thinking. He was still thinking, eyes wide in the darkness, as Cynthia snuggled down to sleep beside him that night.

After a while, he came to a decision. He care-fully slid out of bed so as not to disturb her and dressed in silence. Out in the corridor the lights were dimmed. Mare Stellatis mimicked Earth's diurnal cycle for the benefit of its human charges. He padded down the ring corridor to the nearest intersection, then turned in toward the center of the City. Once there, he climbed the circular ramp to the barren instrument room and through it to the observation dome. It was lunar morning and the sun cast long, stark shadows from the crater rim. The brilliance was painful until his eyes adjusted from the semidarkness of the corridors. He went to the base of the dome, tracking around its inside rim until he found what he was looking for. He looked carefully, then moved a little way and examined another object.

The next day dragged slowly as he mulled over what he had seen and what he intended to do. He knew what he would be abandoning—and he knew there was no good reason to do it. He was driven by ghosts from his past and their shadow darkened his future. Sensibly he should stay, love Cynthia, build a place in the community, put down roots for the first time in his life. He needed that stability more than he cared to admit. Now it was his for the asking, but first he needed redemption, and he couldn't earn it in paradise.

That night he lay with Cynthia after loveplay. He was rubbing her back, caressing her, but his motions were mechanical, his mind was elsewhere. *Should I tell her?* He pondered the question.

There was no good answer. Eventually he made up his mind. "I have to leave, Cyn," he told her.

She looked over her shoulder at him, questioning him with languid eyes. "What, now?"

"I mean leave Mare Stellatis. Get back to the world."

She rolled over and looked at him, no longer relaxed. "You mean escape."

"Yes."

"You're serious?" She was giving him another chance to say no.

He held her gaze. "Yes."

"Why?" She sounded hurt. "Don't you like it here? Don't you like me?"

"I do Cyn, I do, but it's not real. There's no challenge for me here. I don't want to spend the rest of my life cleaning pipes and playing chess."

"But you hated the real world. You told me so yourself."

"I did. I do. But I need it. I can't just wallow in paradise for the rest of my life. I'm not accomplishing anything here."

"And you were accomplishing so much out there." The sarcasm was palpable. She was angry.

"I was surviving."

"You're doing better than that here."

"I'm not doing much of *anything* here."

"Corrective Services will pop the dome; we'll

all die. Unless Vincennes catches you and puts you Downside first." She was trying to talk him out of it.

"Those things won't happen, not if you help me."

"You want *me* to help you?" She laughed. "You *are* out of your mind."

"We can do it together."

"We can't do it together, because *we* aren't doing anything. And neither are you." She said it firmly, as if that would make it true. "Come under the covers and don't upset me with this anymore."

He did as she asked, and held her. Both of them knew it was the last time.

The next day two monitors came for him at the pump room. "Come on, Vincennes wants to see you. Now." The threat was implicit in the man's voice. Tombuol looked at Tyrell questioningly, hefting the heavy wrench he was using to tighten a pump fitting. Tyrell shook his head gently. *He's willing to fight for me. Why? Because I'm his friend, no other reason. I have underestimated him.* He felt a twinge of guilt at his failure to recognize the man's character sooner. To the monitors, he said, "I'm coming." On his way past Tombuol, he offered his hand, then embraced him. The big man watched him go in silence, then turned back to the pump. His expression didn't change, but his emotions showed in the way his muscles strained against the wrench, torquing the fitting far tighter than it needed to go.

The monitors escorted Tyrell up to Vincennes's office, one in front of him on the towcable and one behind. The Coordinator was pacing in front of his desk. Stelchek was standing impassively behind the door. Cynthia was sitting on a chair beside it. She wouldn't meet his gaze. *You betrayed me*, he thought, but he felt pity for her rather than anger. She'd sold herself out long before this. Perhaps she didn't even realize it.

Vincennes stopped pacing and looked at him. "I understand you've been planning an escape." His voice was sharp.

"Not planning one. Thinking about planning one."

"You know what escape means for the rest of us, don't you? You're happy to let us die, is that it?"

"I know how to get out. We can all get out."

"And how is that?" Vincennes's voice dripped sarcasm.

"The vehicle maintenance stations, they have exits to the surface. There might be equipment left over, even vehicles.

The Coordinator laughed. "You think you're the first to look at that map and dream of escape? It's been tried. The map isn't even accurate any more, not even close. Nobody who's gone looking for a maint station has ever come back."

"Maybe they escaped."

"Maybe they froze in the dark. Maybe they're still Downside mining water. Nobody escapes from Mare Stellatis."

"How do you know?" Even as he said it, Tyrell wondered *why do you push him?* "If we all worked together we could find a way through."

"Do you think Corrective Services is stupid? There's no power down those tunnels. They aren't in the convection cycle. No heat, no light. You can get lost in two hundred meters and freeze in an hour. Even if you ever found a maint station, I'm sure you'd find the lock sealed and the equipment stripped."

"But you don't know. Even if the airlocks can't be opened, there'd be equipment we can use."

"There is no equipment and the locks are sealed. It can't be done, Lewis."

"I can do it. *We* can do it." He looked at the faces around him. Stelchek was openly hostile. The monitors were impassively waiting for their leader's command. Cynthia was still avoiding his gaze.

"Nobody is going anywhere." Vincennes

became almost paternal. "I understand the pressure you feel. We've all felt it, it's just built up with you for a while. What you need is some time to think about it."

It was the critical moment. The Coordinator was offering clemency. Tyrell could back down now and it would all be forgotten. It would be easier that way, but he needed to confirm what he'd learned the other night. "I know about the instrument dome." His voice was flat.

"What are you talking about?" Vincennes's voice was sharp again.

"You know exactly what I'm talking about." He kept his voice firm and level.

The Coordinator jerked his head at the guards. "Leave us. Wait outside." When Stelchek hesitated, Vincennes gestured violently. "You too. Now." Checker moved out, shepherding Cynthia.

When they were alone, Vincennes advanced on him. Tyrell stood his ground. "Now, suppose you tell me exactly what you think you know." There was derision in his voice. *He's trying to shake my confidence. And by doing that he proves I am right.*

Instead of answering Lewis asked a question of his own. "You like it here, don't you?"

"What's that got to do with anything?"

"You enjoy ruling paradise. First among

equals—just a little more equal than everyone else. It's a nice setup. But it wouldn't be any fun with no one to rule, would it?"

Vincennes remained silent.

Tyrell went on, the words tumbling forth without thought, driven by an anger he'd been unaware he was harboring. "But what if all your subjects are incorrigibles? Freethinkers and hard-core escape artists? They'll all melt away into the night no matter what the obstacles. Unless you have some way of controlling them. Reward and punishment, Upside and Downside, just like Corrective Services. You hold heaven and hell in either hand, Vincennes. And then you have the ultimate social sanction. Freethinkers will risk their lives to be free. Most people here already have. But who would condemn the whole community to death in an escape attempt? No one that unstable would ever be sent here, C.S. would have them in a treatment center."

Vincennes looked at him steadily. "If you have something to say, I think you better say it."

Tyrell returned his gaze with equanimity. "C.S. isn't watching the basin, Vincennes." His voice was back under control. "There aren't any explosives around the dome. I checked, I know a det-pak when I see one. The seals were taken out to make the convection system work. You and

Stelchek created a myth for social control and you've done better than Corrective Services could have ever hoped. You're a very clever man, Coordinator." *His answer will confirm the truth, but I already know.*

Vincennes studied him for a long moment, then spoke. "You are too dangerous, Captain Lewis Tyrell. I knew that the first time I saw you. I nearly put you Downside the day you arrived. I didn't, but I should have. I'll correct that mistake now."

There was a sudden motion and a tiny darter appeared in his hand. Tyrell threw himself to one side even as Vincennes fired and the dart whipped past his ear. He kicked off the wall and leapt toward Vincennes, grabbing a clipboard as a shield. The other man fired again and the dart *thwacked* into the hard plastic. Tyrell recognized the darter—that model only carried two darts. He threw the clipboard to force Vincennes off balance, then ran into him. They both went down in a flailing heap. It was going to be a wrestling match and the Coordinator's lunar adapted muscles would be no match for Tyrell. An instant later the other man went limp under him and Tyrell put him in a lockhold. It was too easy.

A burning sensation stabbed into his thigh and he felt his leg go numb. He looked down in shock to see a tiny drugdart sticking out of it. Vincennes had stabbed him with a reload round. He looked back into his opponent's face and saw triumph written there. The triumph turned to panic as fighting rage washed over Tyrell and he refastened his hands around Vincennes's throat, squeezing with all his strength. Vincennes tried ineffectually to pry the hands loose. Tyrell watched as the other man's eyes bulged and the fear of death came into his face. But the drug was spreading numbness through his body and he felt his grip weakening. He willed his hands to close but they slowly relaxed and the fear drained from Vincennes's face.

Tyrell's hands fell away and he slumped across the floor. Vincennes struggled to his feet and looked down, rubbing his throat. When he spoke, his voice was hoarse and shaky and Tyrell took satisfaction in that. "Almost, Lewis. Closer than anyone yet. But not quite." He leaned over and pulled the dart out of Tyrell's thigh, then retrieved the other two from the wall and the clipboard. *He keeps his darts a secret,* thought Tyrell. *Uneasy rests the head that bears the crown.*

For a moment Vincennes stood over him, looking down. He seemed about to say something else, then suddenly turned on his heel and left. From the corridor Tyrell heard his voice, overloud but in better control than it had been. "He attacked me and he lost. Dump him down the mine."

Tyrell's muscular control had returned by the time they carried him to the bottom of the City. They used stairs rather than slide poles, presumably to prevent him from trying to escape. He could have anyway—despite their caution, their stunrods, and the hidden threat of Vincennes's darter—but he didn't bother to try. The maint stations weren't accessible from Upside, they were at the end of the mining tunnels beneath it. If he wanted to escape, Downside was the only way to go. Vincennes hadn't needed force.

Or perhaps he had. Tyrell had intended to take Cynthia with him. If he could have planned openly he would have taken others as well. As a group, they would have demanded supplies and equipment. A concerted search for an escape route driven by Tyrell would have undermined the Coordinator's position. Upside ventures into the Downside tunnels would have changed the power balance in Mare Stellatis. Tyrell's knowledge of the truth behind the instrument dome was reason enough for Vincennes's precautions. The Coordinator was simply maintaining the status quo.

The air was cooler at the bottom level, sixteen or seventeen Celsius, he judged, and the steady breeze down the ventshafts made it feel colder still. They took him to the same hatchway he'd helped carry food to. The monitors unbolted it and hauled it open. It took two of them even under lunar gravity. He hadn't noticed how massive it was before.

Vincennes gestured and the guards pushed him to the brink. No choice. *Not even if they weren't here*, he realized. He had been committed to this step since he'd arrived, without even realizing it. He stepped over the edge and fell. His fall took too long, and for a single panicked instant he thought that there was no Downside—that the black hole he was falling into was just a deep pit, the bottom covered with the shattered bodies of Upsider dissidents. Then his feet hit the ground and he collapsed in a heap, bruised but intact. Twenty or so meters above him he could see the circle of light that marked the hole he had fallen through. There was a loud *clang* and the grating broke up the light. He heard the bolts shoot home, and then silence.

Tyrell's first awareness of Downside was the temperature. It was cool in the rock chamber. Cool and dark. Energy was the currency of Mare Stellatis. Here there was less. Downsiders survived on the dregs Upside cared to drop on them. As his eyes adapted to the darkness, he took stock of his surroundings. The chamber was an irregular circle, perhaps three meters across. Illumination came from glowing green tritium lights set at intervals along the walls. The rock on the floor beneath him was textured in shallow, parallel grooves—clearly the toolmarks of whatever huge mining machine had dug it.

"Welcome to hell."

Tyrell spun around, startled by the voice.

"Welcome to hell, newling." The man repeated himself and a dark shape emerged from the shadows. His words were an eerie echo of Stelchek's greeting upon his arrival at Mare Stellatis.

"Lewis Tyrell." He offered his hand.

The other man ignored it. "Are you fit?"

"I keep myself in shape." There was something else. He sensed rather than saw other figures in the chamber. *Danger here.*

"That's not an answer."

Tyrell shrugged and remained silent. After a moment, the questions continued.

"Are you smart?"

"Smart enough." There were two others, standing quietly but occasional small noises betrayed their presence. Guards, waiting for a command from their leader. *Their muscles are adapted to lunar gravity. I can beat them.*

"We'll see. Do you have any skills?

"I was an infantry officer during the war."

"What was your rank?"

"Captain." *Unless they have weapons.*

"Well Captain Tyrell, let me explain the situation to you. This is the real Mare Stellatis. Here we mine water. The Upsiders give us supplies, *if* we meet our quotas. There's no slack for someone who can't pull his weight. Here you work, or you die."

"I can do that." *Show caution. Don't offer challenge.*

"We'll see. Work hard and life can be acceptable. Slack off and—" he finished the sentence with an open-handed gesture.

"When do I start?"

"Right now. I'm Checker." The man caught Tyrell's surprised expression in the gloom. "Downside Checker. You'll learn the difference, if it isn't already clear."

"Is there a Coordinator down here as well."

"We don't have enough people to go around as it is. Any organizing that needs doing, I do it. You can call me Coordinator if you like it better. You can call me any damn thing you please, and sooner or later you probably will. I don't care, just so long as you dig your quota."

"Where do I start?"

"Go that way, soldier." Checker pointed down a dim tunnel, away from the concealed guards. "Ask for Myzer."

Tyrell moved off in the direction indicated. As he reached the tunnel entrance he had to step back. A woman, muscles rippling beneath gaunt skin, was pushing a crude cart overflowing with chunks of rock. The cart passed and he moved on. Behind him he overheard words.

"Whatcha got, Skyly?"

"I make it six hundred kilos, Checker."

The rest of the conversation was lost in the darkness. As he moved forward, he found the tunnel illuminated by more than the irregular glow of the tritium glow lamps. Faint smears of red light showed in the darker shadows. He stopped to investigate, rubbing his finger on a patch. The patch felt damp and the glow came away, stuck to his finger. He examined it closely under a tritium light and saw nothing but black slime. Some kind of luminous fungus, then. He wiped his finger clean and went on. The air grew noticeably colder as he moved farther down the tunnel. *No insulation, rapid heat loss. It will be cold in the outer tunnels.* He would have to travel those tunnels to reach one of the surface maintenance stations. Before he could do that, he would need to learn just how cold they were and find a way to keep himself warm.

Soon he heard sounds of work and voices. He followed them and found two women and three men digging at the rock face with picks and loading the ore into a cart similar to the one he'd seen before. He approached the closest figure, a stocky man, powerfully muscled for the lunar gravity. He was overseeing the loading.

"Excuse me, I'm looking for Myzer." *Show no threat.*

"I'm Myzer." It was noticeably colder than the chamber where he'd met Checker and the air was damp and musty.

"I'm Tyrell. I'm to work with you."

The man gestured. "Extra pick over there, Tyrell."

"What do I do?"

Myzer pointed at the rock face, where two more figures were swinging picks with a steady, measured rhythm. "You mine ice-ore, like this stuff, see." He hefted a chunk of gray rock. "Load it in the trolley."

"How do I move ahead?" *Learn the system.*

Myzer laughed without humor. "Ambitious, aren't you?"

Tyrell shrugged.

"Understand the reality here." Myzer held up a hand. "Ninety percent of us work sixteen hours a day at the bore face to meet the quota. Everyone else is directly involved in supporting that effort. You were ahead when you were Upside. You want to impress me, you mine a lot of water."

Tyrell fell back on what had worked with Checker. "I can do that."

"Understand the reality, newling. Fail to pull your weight and you're outcast. That means you die. That's the way it is here. Dig hard."

Wordlessly, Tyrell picked up the pick and fell into place between the two figures at the bore face. The woman fell back to give him room, the man paused for a moment. "Name's Thorven. Dig ice here." He indicated a vein of the grayish rock Myzer had shown him. The ice-ore itself was porous, like dense pumice, saturated with water locked into its structure by temperature and pressure.

Water dripped from the vein and there were puddles on the floor beneath his feet. Tyrell swung his pick and it bit into the rock. Suddenly anger welled up in him—anger at Vincennes and the Upsiders who lived in paradise atop this hell, anger at Corrective Services who'd devised the diabolical system in the first place and the SIS who'd consigned him to it. Anger at the Judas comrade who had betrayed him. Anger at himself for his failures. He channeled the rage and frustration into each stroke, taking pleasure in the shock of impact as it bit into the rock. He swung again and again, savagely, heedless of the way the pick handle tore at his hands. Blisters formed and burst but he kept swinging, ignoring the pain.

Somewhere along the line a hand on his shoulder brought him up short. His muscles were sore and he was unsure how much time had passed. He looked up from the bore face and found one of the women looking at him from the darkness. "Angela," she said. "My shift."

Tyrell suddenly realized that tears were streaming down his face. *How long have I buried this rage?* he wondered, thinking back to his encounter with Vincennes. The action was so unlike him that it seemed he must be examining someone else's memories. Captain Lewis Tyrell had killed before, with maximum violence and without mercy. He had done it as many times as duty demanded, but never had he *wanted* to kill simply for its own sake. Mare Stellatis had triggered something in him, something he didn't know how to control. He remembered how he had wanted to see Vincennes die, choke out his life with his own hands. It went against everything he had taught himself. *Emotional control is the key.* But a key can both open and close a lock.

The woman pulled him aside, ignoring the expression on his face. "My shift," she repeated firmly. He saw that Myzer had taken Thorven's place and was swinging with powerful, regular strokes. Wordlessly, he handed Angela the pick and stumbled away. She took up a rhythm syncopated with Myzer's, metal ringing against rock with a steady *ching, ching, ching.*

Thorven was loading ice-ore onto the trolley. The other man and woman were digging a seam farther up the tunnel. Without waiting to be asked, Tyrell moved up behind them and started hauling ice-ore back to Thorven. There was a rhythm to the work, a pattern. As each person tired at the bore face, another moved up to take over. Loading the ore on the trolley was hardly less work than swinging a pick, but it was a different motion, different muscles. Eventually the trolley was full and the crew took a break while Tyrell helped Myzer wheel it down the tunnel. The lunar gravity allowed the trolley to carry an incredible amount of rock and still move, but its inertia was unchanged and it was difficult to maneuver it down the rough-floored tunnel. Tyrell developed new respect for the woman he'd seen pushing her cart single-handed.

When they reached the chamber beneath the grating, he learned how the ice-ore was refined. The process was simplicity itself. Checker and his guard/assistants weighed the load on a crude overhead scale and applied the tally for Myzer. After that, the trolley—now sloshing with water melted out of the ore—was simply dumped down a pit twenty meters beyond the spot where Tyrell had

fallen. A line of glowlamps marked the edge of the
pit. Its bottom and far edge were invisible in the
gloom. When they dropped the load in, there was
no answering thud from the bottom of the shaft,
although Tyrell listened for long seconds. Whatever noise the load made was lost on the steady
breeze that blew against his back and down the
shaft. While he was trying to gauge the depth of
the pit, Myzer and Checker exchanged a few
words out of his earshot. *Comparing notes, assess-
ing me*, he thought, but made no move to try and
eavesdrop. He would learn their opinions soon
enough. When they were done talking, Myzer
waved him over and they started pushing the cart
back to the bore face.

Myzer explained the system on the way. The
pit was actually a ventshaft, performing the same
function as the ones in the City. It was one of several in the mine that formed the back half of Mare
Stellatis's convection cycle. As soon as the rock
was relieved of the pressure from the lunar over-
burden the ice began to melt out. Down the shaft,
the relatively warmer air flowing past helped the
process. The water and oxygen both filtered
through the accumulation of fractured rock to an
underground stream that eventually came out in
the Watercave in the Garden.

Hope surged in Tyrell's chest for a moment.

"That means there must be a path from here to the Garden."

Myzer laughed. "If you think you can get out that way, you go ahead and try. It's more than a thousand meters down that shaft and you haven't got a pole to slide down either. Lunar gravity or not, that fall will kill you. But if you manage to make it down, there you are, home free. You've only got about ten years' accumulation of rock to dig through. While the rest of us dump our daily quota on your head."

"But there's got to be more than one airshaft," Tyrell objected.

"Sure there is, but this is the closest one to the Watercave. If you get down another one you'll still have to dig your way past the spoil. Air and water can get through. Maybe a lizard could, if there were any lizards in this godforsaken hole. Anything bigger is a vanishing dream."

The crew was still resting when they got back. Myzer introduced him to the other man and woman. "Flame and Smythe." Tyrell raised a hand and they nodded in affirmation.

"Lewis Tyrell," he said, perhaps unnecessarily.

Angela passed him a fused stone jug full of water. Under earth's gravity it would have been awkwardly large. "Drink," she encouraged. "You'll need it."

Conversation lagged as they passed the jug around. Tyrell felt himself growing chill without the exertion to warm him.

"Checker tells me you're a soldier," Myzer said when they were done. The others were moving back to pick up their tools.

"I was, a long time ago."

"You worked hard, soldier. You impressed me." *He waited until we were back to say this,* thought Tyrell. *He's saying it for the others, not me.* Myzer was still talking. "How long since you came to Mare Stellatis?"

"Not long. A couple of months."

"You still have Earth muscles. That's good. One more shift and then we eat." He clapped Tyrell on the back. *Acceptance.* Lewis picked up a pick and began digging, feeling the pain in his hands where the blisters had started to bleed.

The shift was long. By the end of it, Tyrell's muscles ached to the bone. He didn't know how it was that Myzer knew when to call a halt, but eventually he did. The crew filed back to the chamber beneath the air vent in silence. Some crews were already there standing in line. Tyrell's group joined them and others fell in behind them. Checker and two other women were there, handing out packages of food. Myzer was at the front of the group, Tyrell was at the back behind

Angela and Thorven. He overheard the man behind him complaining and paused to catch the conversation.

"Short rations today, Checker." The man's voice was neutral.

"Short cubic, Stolly." Checker's reply was flat.

"My vein is running a little short, you know. Cut us some line, Checker." A hint of a whine had crept into Stolly's voice.

"You know the rules."

Stolly sighed. "I know. I invoke exploration privilege."

"Not this time, Stolly."

"Please, Checker." The whine was more pronounced.

"I can't. You know it and I know it."

"I know." The whine was gone. The man sounded resigned.

"Your luck will change. Keep trying." Checker's voice was more animated, encouraging. There was no reply from Stolly.

Tyrell caught up to the figures receding in the dimness in front of him and nudged Thorven. "What's exploration privilege?"

"Stolly claim it, did he?"

"Yah." Tyrell unwrapped his food package, revealing a cake of pounded grain and strips of dried chinchilla meat.

"It's like this. Ice-ore comes in pockets. When your pocket runs out you have to find a new one, or dig through the seam to the next one. So the team leader gets two days, six meals, to go looking while his crew digs. We'll carry them for that time, two days in thirty, max. After that, it's up to them. The leader's crew can carry him awhile, if they decide they want to keep him as leader, and if they've got the ore to do it. Stolly's had bad luck for some time now. He might not make it this time."

"Checker wouldn't give him exploration privilege."

"It's too soon after that last time. Too bad. It's up to his crew now."

"What if they decide they don't want him?"

"They'll go join other crews if any will take them, or choose another leader and work without him."

"And if not?"

"We look after our own as much as we can, soldier. But if you don't make quota, you can't eat. That's just a fact. Stay on top of your production or you'll starve. It's that simple." Thorven bit into his food, ending the conversation.

After eating, they filed into a cavernous room beneath another barred ventshaft from Upside. The floor was covered in straw, providing some meager insulation from the cold rock beneath. By sleeping in groups, the Downsiders conserved body heat. Men and women jumbled together indiscriminately. Tyrell wound up pressed between Myzer and Flame, but there was no hint of sexuality in the situation. Even if she'd offered an invitation, he was simply too exhausted to respond.

The lack of a day-night cycle was disorienting and Tyrell's existence became an unending blur of work, eat, and sleep. Sleep and food were the parameters that defined the work environment. Sixteen hours to quota was the target all the crew chiefs aimed to beat. More than sixteen hours meant you were losing sleep or calories. Either one meant you were on the wrong side of the slope. Your efficiency would drop and next time you'd get less. An isolated lapse could be made up with superhuman efforts next shift, but any steady problem meeting quota in time led to a downward spiral with only one ending.

There was a rhythm to the work. Pulling with an even strain, Myzer called it. Expending too much effort at once cut into efficiency, both in terms of cubic mined and calories expended. Myzer's crew worked fifteen hours with an hour for eating and eight for sleep. It was more than they needed to work—they had a good vein and met the quota in fourteen hours, but Myzer was building a reserve against the day they would face hard times.

There was little talk at the bore face and none at all during sleep periods. What Tyrell learned, he learned during meals. The composition of a crew was a subject of much debate. Too small a group couldn't work efficiently and would fall behind on their quotas. Too large a group ate up ore pockets quickly and lost more time looking for new ones. Some crew leaders favored women because their greater endurance and cold tolerance let them produce more ice for fewer calories. Others preferred men because their strength let them dig more ore in less time. Ultimately it came down to the rapport the crew members had with each other. A good crew working in a good pocket could generate five cubic meters of ore per member in as little as twelve hours. A poor crew in a poor pocket couldn't do it in eighteen.

Another important parameter was the distance from a crew's bore face to the ventshafts. The shafts were the only source of heat in Downside. There were four in addition to the one used for ore dumping, arranged in a rough semicircle and connected by tunnels about two hundred meters long. Within this area the temperature was tolerable. A steady, gentle breeze blew out from this core area down the mining tunnels and warmed them, but it became rapidly colder as you moved outward. Mining a pocket a hundred meters from the ventshafts was tolerable. Two hundred meters past that the temperature dropped to near freezing. Another two hundred meters marked the limit of Downside's usable zone, beyond that it was simply to cold to work. Closer mining sites also meant a shorter haul for the ice trolleys. Over the years, the close-in sites had become exhausted and digging in Downside had become progressively harder.

Once during a meal break Tyrell asked Checker what he'd done to get himself banished.

"That's a pretty personal question, soldier."

"Just making conversation, Checker, no strain if you don't answer."

Checker considered him for a long moment. "You met Vincennes?"

"Yah."

"Let's just say I'd rather rule in hell than serve in heaven."

"I hear you there."

There was a lull in the conversation as they both ate. Then Tyrell said, "I've been thinking. If we could get Upside, we could take over. They're soft up there, no one would stand against us."

"Yah, and how do propose to do that? Those bars will bounce your pick like it was made of rubber. They don't just cover the opening, you know, they're set in the rock right across the bottom of the City."

"We could try. What have we got to lose?"

"Food, for one thing. Listen, if you've got spare calories to bang a rock on those bars, you go right ahead. Just don't cry to me when the monitors rap your fingers with a shockrod. Forget it, soldier."

Tyrell let the conversation drop, but later on he brought the subject up with Thorven.

"Look," he said, after Thorven had echoed Checker's explanation about the bars. "They open that hatch once a day to lower food and supplies. That's when they're vulnerable."

"They know that too, Lewis." The big man was unimpressed. "They're ready for anything like that."

"Nobody can stay ready forever. We just need to surprise them and we're in."

"Hmm . . . Maybe."

Tyrell didn't push the point with Thorven right away. Instead, he made a point of talking to Flame about it. She was more enthusiastic and he worked on her. Together they worked on Thorven and started on Myzer. *Sooner or later, Checker will have to take notice.*

It turned out to be sooner. Seven shifts after their first conversation, a Downsider he knew by face but not by name came over to where Myzer's crew was eating. "Hey Lewis," he called. "Checker wants to see you." He pointed across the chamber. Tyrell swallowed the last couple of bites of his meal and went over.

Checker stood up when he saw Tyrell, but his manner was relaxed. "Seems you're trying to start a revolution, soldier. You want to go to war with Upside?"

"I'm not going to stay down here mining ice while they swim in the hot springs."

"Y'know, you're getting things kind of stirred up. We can't really afford a lot of strife down here. Any little problem starts to hurt the quota and we all suffer."

"Maybe it's time we changed that. Maybe things need stirring up."

Checker's manner changed. He stood up and moved in close, crowding Tyrell. "Take a long look at me. You think I'm a coward?"

Threat posture. He's trying to dominate or force me to fight. Tyrell didn't back down or rise to the bait; he just shook his head slowly. "No."

Checker relaxed slightly, but didn't move away either. "Damn right I'm not. Nobody gets down here for cowardice. Nobody. If I thought we could take out Upside I'd do it tomorrow. I'd do it if half of us died in the process."

"Then let's do it. Put some of them down here for a change."

"You don't understand, soldier. They outnumber us ten to one. That doesn't scare me, but they've also got us down here. That *does* scare me. We have got one chance. *One.* Then they lock down that grating and they don't unlock it until we've all starved. Vincennes and Stelchek won't bat an eyelash. They'll just grab the bottom two hundred Upsiders and drop them down here instead. Work 'em twice as hard for a couple of months to make up the water reserve they use while they're waiting us out."

People started to take note of the conversation and move closer to hear. Tyrell raised his voice slightly for their benefit. "It's worth the risk. Anything is better than this."

"You're probably right, soldier, but I'm responsible for two hundred people here. I'd take that one chance if I thought I could make it work, but I don't." Checker had raised his voice, too.

"Then we can escape, find one of the surface maint stations and get a vehicle to Farside."

"We'll have three days to find it. That's how long it takes the ore down the shaft to melt out. After that, our rations are gone. You going to promise me you can find a vehicle in three days? And make it work? And get two hundred people to Farside in it? You going to guarantee that will happen, soldier? What do I get if you're wrong?"

You get death, we all do. The imperative of group survival. It was the same argument Vincennes had used. Except in Checker's case, it wasn't a fiction manufactured to allow control, it was simple reality.

"I can't promise anything."

Checker leaned back and spread his arms, addressing the crowd. "Well people, pay attention to what he's selling you. *Nothing!*" he leaned close again. "Know this, Tyrell. I'd try your plan it if had a snowball's chance in hell of working. I'd lead a revolt against Upside on less chance than that. The fact is, there is no chance. I don't appreciate being second guessed."

"The maint stations are out there. The vehicles are out there. I can find them."

"You believe that, do you?"

"I believe I have to try. Give me exploration privilege and I'll get us all out."

Checker shook his head. "Maint stations aren't one pockets. You couldn't get to the tunnel head in two days even if you knew where you were going. You'd freeze the first night."

"Give me the chance, Checker."

"You've got your chance, just no exploration privileges. We don't have enough margin here for dissenters—that's just the way it is. Nothing personal. You're out of here, soldier. You're outcast. Get going."

Wordlessly Tyrell turned and left, feeling the eyes of the silent crowd on them. *Why did I push the issue? I forced him to throw me out.* He quickly left the dim circle of light shed by the tritium lamps and moved into the darkness of the unlit outer tunnel. Checker's voice came after him. "Hey soldier! Good luck!" He sounded as if he meant it.

Tyrell didn't go far, just a few hundred meters. Then he waited quietly. Eventually, the noises filtering down the tunnel told him the group had left the lit area. He waited longer. Patience was a skill driven home by countless long patrols. Finally, when he was sure the way was clear, he stealthily moved back, making sure that no one was waiting for him in the shadows. It was the work of a moment to pry a glow lamp loose from the wall and hide it under his sweater. Then he turned and left. The Downsiders had nothing for him now, but he needed light to see his way through the outer tunnels to the exit he knew was waiting for him. That was his first goal. Once he achieved it, he'd have to figure out how to cross a couple hundred kilometers of rugged terrain, in vacuum, without the benefit of any equipment whatsoever. The prospect did not daunt him. He felt an odd kind of inspiration. All his bridges were burned now, for better or for worse. He was thrice cast out and he would live or die on no one's word but his own.

There was only one way to go, and that was down. He set off at a jog trot, keeping the wind at his back. It was the only way to navigate—if it would work. Perhaps others who'd been consigned to this icy, dark hell had made the same decision. There was no way of knowing. There were hundreds of kilometers of corridors but he could move fast in the low lunar gravity. Somewhere, he knew, there had to be a way out. He called up the image of the map in his mind's eye, striving to remember the route to the other entrance to Mare Stellatis, woven through the spaghetti tangle of mine tunnels. Once he had it pictured, he set off, hoping against hope that he could navigate the complex path in the dark. He came to a tunnel junction and chose the one that seemed to go straightest. He had hoped to navigate by using the direction of the convective breeze, but once he left the ventshafts behind the air was perfectly still. He came to another junction and chose again. The tunnels were curved and he couldn't be sure he was maintaining direction.

Hours later, he had to admit he was lost. The air was cold and he was growing hungry. He tried scraping some of the glowfungus from the wall with his fingernails, but half an hour of effort yielded less than a thimbleful of bitter slime. His body fat was already low from his work mining ice-ore. He needed calories.

Beyond that, he needed a way out. He was fit and healthy, he could live on muscle mass for a while. He wouldn't freeze as long as he could keep moving. Sleep was risky. Maybe not the first night, maybe not the second, but as his energy reserves dwindled hypothermia would eventually claim him. He needed to escape before that happened. He needed to keep moving. The only question was, which direction.

He pictured the map again. There were hundreds of kilometers of tunnels. There was no way he could search them all before he died, but if he could get to a landmark, an elevator shaft or a service junction, it might help him navigate. The first problem was to find one of them. The answer was clear, if discouraging. He would go down each tunnel and turn left at every junction. Sooner or later he would come back to his starting point, and in the meantime he would walk every meter of the tunnel system he was in. If he came back to where he started he'd go to the next junction, turn right and then repeat the process. If he found a service junction he would explore it. Surely the mining machinery must have had some method of navigating. Even if it didn't, the people who came to tend it must have. If he could figure it out he would be home free.

Plan made. He gathered a few stray hunks of rock into a cairn to mark his start point, chose his direction, and fell into an efficient, long-stepped stride. The patches of glowfungus provided just enough light to pick his next two steps. It was like the infantry all over again, picking his way through darkness and unfamiliar terrain. Here at least he had the light of the glow lamp to guide him. As he walked, fragments of an old poem ran through his mind. *For I have promises to keep, and miles to go before I sleep.*

Four hours later, he'd lost track of the number of cairns he'd made and eventually come back to. He had stopped to build another one when he noticed something. It was a breeze—cool, steady, and moist. It had to be going somewhere. Either he'd traveled in a huge circle and was back at the ventshafts or he'd discovered something important. Either way the moving air provided a steady navigation reference he could use to make some real progress. He pondered whether to travel with or against the wind. The answer depended on where it was coming from, of course. The most likely explanation was that it was blowing from the ventshafts, in which case he should move downwind and away from them, but there was also the chance that this was a rogue current coming out the back of the main convection cycle through the Watercave and circulating through the bottom tunnels. On consideration he favored the second option. The moisture in the wind hinted at the Watercave and he'd come down many levels and traveled a long way from the ventshafts in his journey. Myzer said nothing larger than a lizard could make it through to the Watercave, but Myzer had never tried. If he could get through, he'd be able to eat and sleep in the Garden at night, hiding out from the Upsiders in the tunnels during the day. With no worries about food or warmth, he could explore the tunnels systematically and sooner or later he *would* succeed.

He set off with renewed hope and energy. He'd traveled perhaps a kilometer before disaster struck. The passage had suddenly become a sharp downgrade. As he made his way down he suddenly slipped and slid uncontrollably. The rough rock tore at his clothes and flesh, until he crashed to a halt at the bottom—in half a meter of ice water, the splash echoing emptily against the tunnel walls. He gasped at the cold, then instinctively stood up to get his body core up before the water could steal any more precious heat. It was too late, the damage was done. His clothing was soaked. In the cold darkness of the tunnels it would never dry, and hypothermia would come quickly. He stripped off the sodden garments, but that was only delaying the inevitable. Without protection, he would die. And meanwhile, his feet and calves were getting painfully cold. More heat loss. He tried to climb out of the shallow pool, but the passage he'd slid down was too steep and slippery to climb up. Desperate, he fell flat on his belly and tried to worm his way out of the water. Each time the icy slope defeated him, drenching him again in the frigid pool.

It was clear there was no future in that. He'd have to go forward and hope the water didn't get any deeper. And that it ended quickly.

Easier to rest. He was so tired, so cold. Sleep was a seductive option. He fought off the lethargy. That was hypothermia, already extending its icy fingers into his brain and sapping his will. He forced his way ahead on frozen feet. The water had a thin crust of ice on it that broke against his shins in razor shards. It felt as though it was cutting him, and in the dark he couldn't tell if the moisture on his legs was water or his own blood. It didn't matter. He had to get out, and then somehow get dry and warm.

By the time he reached the other end of the

pool he was shaking uncontrollably. He didn't try to stop the shivering, he knew his body was doing its best to generate heat. The pool ended in a blank wall. Directly above his head a vertical shaft led straight up, but there was no way he could climb it. Air flowed down the shaft, feeling slightly warmer than the air in the corridor had. It wouldn't be enough to save him, though, not with the water sucking calories from his body faster than he could generate them. He had to go back.

The return journey was endless. He had to concentrate on each step. Some part of his brain kept telling him to give it up, to surrender to the peaceful sleep waiting for him. He fought it back, but that made it hard to concentrate on his steps. He hit his foot against something underwater. There was no pain, his feet were totally numb, but he pitched forward into the pool. He came up gasping and shivering. He tried to stand but couldn't and fell forward again, inhaling water. His legs wouldn't work, and now his arms were disobeying him as well. He struggled to get his torso clear of the frigid water. Instead he fell over sideways, breathing more water. Again he tried to force himself upright, but nothing worked. He felt himself stop shivering, and then sleep and delicious warmth descended, and he surrendered himself to welcome oblivion.

CHAPTER THREE

RESURRECTION

A TIMELESS TIME PASSED and he was still warm, although somehow he knew he should be dead. Perhaps he was—perhaps death was simply eternal, dreamy warmth, like sleep. A comforting echo of the womb. He tried to hang on to the thought, but it drifted away. He slipped in and out of fevered, confused dreams. At times he was aware he was dreaming but was unable to escape to wakefulness. At other times there was nothing but blissful unconsciousness. Occasionally a nameless choking terror seized him and he surfaced to what seemed like the real world only to have that reality dissolve into tenuous dream strands again.

Eventually he moved into normal slumber, and consciousness slowly resolved into awareness. He was in a bed under thick blankets. The room was dimly lit with patches of glowfungus on the walls. It was warm beneath the covers, but the air was cool and smelled dank. *I am alive*, he thought. *I have been saved—or has it all been a dream?* But the glowfungus was real and the dank smell of Downside pervasive—it was no dream. He sat up in bed and the rush of cold air beneath the sheets served to banish the last wisps of sleep.

"You're awake." He started. It was a female voice. His eyes found the source, a figure seated against the far wall, bundled in blankets.

"Who are you?" He couldn't think of anything more original to say.

"I'm Jania. Doctor Jania Sycel, if it means anything to you. Try to rest now." She got up and came over to his bedside. "You're past the worst of it."

He ignored her instructions. "Where am I?"

"In Mare Stellatis, of course."

"But *where* in Mare Stellatis?"

"To be exact, you're in maint station 7D in the mining tunnels. You're downside of Downside."

"I thought nothing could live down here."

"I manage. You will too, perhaps, if you rest now." She got up to leave. "I'll bring you some food later."

He tried to get up to follow her and found he lacked the strength. There was nothing to do but lie back and wait. Eventually sleep claimed him again, this time deep, dreamless, and restful.

He awoke again when she turned on the lights. The implications hit him at once. *Lights*

Downside! She has a power source. She had brought him a bowl of steaming soup and its aroma was compelling. The bowl was a glass lens from some light fixture. The soup was rich and full of large vegetable chunks. He devoured it hurriedly, feeling the nourishment spread through his bloodstream almost at once. She brought him a second bowl, which he ate more slowly. In the light he could make out her features. She was in her mid-thirties, he estimated, with hair that fell below her shoulders and shaded from auburn to dark brown depending on where the light hit it. Her eyes too seemed to change color, from green to blue to gray.

"How did I get here?" he asked between bites.

"You fell into my collecting pool. I found you and dragged you out. I thought you were dead at first."

"Your what?"

"My collecting pool. Warm, moist air falls down a shaft from Upside. As it gets colder, the moisture condenses out and drips into my pool."

"You live . . . down here?"

"If live is what you want to call it. I exist."

"How?"

"I get water from condensate, power from the wind. The condensate leaches minerals out of the rock and the power gives me heat and light. That gives me food from my hydroponics garden. I don't need anything else."

"Is there anyone else down here?"

"Now there's you. No one else."

Tyrell was silent. *She set this up alone and unaided. That speaks of formidable determination and resourcefulness.*

She took the empty bowl away from him. "Now you can tell me how you got into my pool in the first place."

"I was trying to escape."

"Nobody escapes Mare Stellatis, and down is the wrong direction anyway."

"I had no choice but to try."

"Why?"

"I was outcast from Downside."

"Why?"

"For trying to escape."

"How did you wind up Downside in the first place?"

He shrugged. "I tried to escape."

She laughed. "You don't seem to learn quickly. Why were you sent to Mare Stellatis? Too many escapes from rehabilitation colonies?"

"No."

"Then why?"

"It's a long story."

"We have nothing but time."

He couldn't argue with that. He told her of his mission and its failure, of how he tried to complete it anyway and how the end of the war robbed him of the chance. How he had saved the vial of Hype as a symbol and how it had led to his arrest for another man's crime. He found himself lost in the telling, relating his experience more for his own benefit than hers. She seemed to recognize this and allowed him to talk without questions or interruptions. At last he finished, and the silence stretched out.

Eventually she spoke. "I'm glad you told me that."

"Why?"

"Did you ever learn what Hype was?"

"No."

"It was—or rather *is*, because Hype and its derivatives are still being developed—a neural interface generator. Nanomachines in a support broth. They literally rebuild brain circuits to allow a human mind to interface with a computer."

"Impossible!"

She shook her head. "I wish you were right, but it's very possible, I assure you. It won the war for the Alliance by allowing real-time human control of computerized combat systems."

"How do you know this?"

"Because I worked at Terradyne during the

war. I was a systems designer. I built the machine side of the man-machine interface. I was one of the scientists you were sent to kill."

Tyrell was silent for a moment. *What can I say? That it was war? That I am sorry?* Instead he said, "How did you wind up here?"

"Hype has serious side effects, as I'm sure you can imagine. Rewiring a living brain is not to be done lightly. Not the least of these side effects is death. The micromachines build their own network within the cortex. As soon as they're finished, the network starts to break up, taking the cortex with it. For a short period there is a useful interface, then the subject's thought functions begin to degrade. Within two weeks, the disintegrating fragments interfere with brain processes enough to kill the subject."

She was speaking to herself as much as to him. *I'm not the only one to bring ghosts to Mare Stellatis,* he thought.

"At first we experimented on animals. Rats, then pigs, finally primates. There was pressure to move to humans. I objected, but of course it was war. Specifically, it was a war of attrition and the U.N. was slowly winning. The government was desperate for anything that might turn the tide. My responsibility was the computer hardware, anyway—it was out of my area. I was overridden."

Tyrell remained silent, nodding to encourage her to continue.

"Again, we started slow. First we used radiation victims who were going to die anyway. There was no shortage of those at the time. Then we used convicted traitors, spies, deserters. That worked until we needed to test interfaces to combat systems. Then we had to move to military volunteers. They weren't told what would happen to them. Need I say I objected? Need I say I was overruled again? I couldn't quit; it was war. A few extra deaths meant nothing against a balance sheet in the hundreds of millions. That was the phase we were at when your attack came. It set us back, and I was glad of it." She looked at him, her face an expressionless mask. "Maybe I should be grateful to you." She paused as if waiting for a response. When none came, she went on.

"It didn't make a difference in the end, of course. Hype was deployed and used. The war ended very quickly after that. In the process, a starship discovered something—something that made Hype very important. I never learned what it was, but the research continued, this time using combat stress patients. No shortage of them either. They were told the Hype interface protocol was a new pschyotreatment. I objected, of course." The bitterness showed in her voice.

"I was overruled again, but this time the war was over. I quit. They tried to convince me to stay, offered me money, equipment, anything I wanted. I told them I wanted the blood washed from my hands. On the day I cleaned out my desk, they arrested me. The day after that I was here. I was lucky. On the way up I learned they'd considered making me a research subject. That might even have been justice of a sort." She looked up, back from her reverie.

"Why did they banish you from Upside?" Tyrell asked.

"They didn't banish me; I came on my own. I didn't want to live in paradise with blood on my hands. I need to atone for my part of what was done. This is my penance."

"War has its own requirements." He was trying to comfort her, but he knew the realities of war had never absolved him of his own guilt.

She shook her head violently. "You've never seen someone undergo the procedure. Hype builds an interface site in the occipital lobe. I designed the hardware to connect to it. They would lase into the site and wire the patient up. The software—*my* software—would map the brainpaths. Conditioning to the interface we called it. We had total control over the subject, like having someone's soul in the palm of your hand." Her voice shook. "I built an induction link to avoid the surgery. That's what we deployed to the field, but in the lab they always went into the brain. With the surgical link they could literally download the entire persona. That made the experiments repeatable." Tears were welling up in her eyes. "The patient would die. You could watch the identity break up into fragments—hallucinations, memory loss. There was always a point when the patients realized what was happening to them. You could see it in their eyes. A few days later there would be nothing but a blank stare. The mind was already dead, but the body would live for days after that, until the Hype got into the medulla and shut off respiration. It didn't matter by then. They—*we*—had the download online. They ran tests you could never perform on a real brain. They dissected living minds, over and over again."

Tyrell remained silent. He had nothing to say. She put her head in her hands, hiding her tears from him. He moved to comfort her and nearly fell over as he tried to stand. When he recovered from the momentary dizziness, she'd gotten up and run out. He didn't try to follow.

The next day he was recovered enough to walk without difficulty. Neither spoke of their conversation the previous day. Both had exposed wounds that ran deep, feelings that didn't bear exposure in normal social intercourse. At first the atmosphere was slightly tense, but as she showed him around it grew more relaxed. Her living space was small—bedroom, living room/kitchen, and storage room. Tyrell had been sleeping in the only bed. All the rooms were insulated with extra layers of sprayfoam and she had a surprising collection of tools and furniture, much of it clearly modified or handmade. Beyond the living area, there was a cold cellar—nothing more than the unheated tunnel beyond her kitchen space. Another tunnel served as her backyard, filled with sundry junk and equipment.

"Where did you get all this?" he asked her.

"Maint stations, mostly. The deeper ones weren't stripped. The most important thing I got was sprayfoam. Insulation was essential for the hydroponic garden."

"Can I see it?"

"Certainly."

The garden was through another door off the kitchen. It was a long tunnel, insulated with sprayfoam and closed off at both ends. Suntubes ran down the center of the roof. Water flowed from a pipe at one end through a series of channels cut into the floor. A pit at the start of the watercourse held organic waste. As it decomposed, it was carried along to nourish the fruits and vegetables growing from metal frames over the channels.

"This is impressive. You did this all yourself?"

"Yes. Thank you," she said, obviously proud of her work. "Of course, I've been improving it for a long time. It wasn't always like this."

He gestured at the suntubes. "Where do you get your power?"

"Come on and I'll show you."

She went back to the back yard and picked up a tritium spotlight. Its glow guided them past the lighted area to a cross tunnel, following a heavy power cable. From there they went up a steel-runged ladder and then down a tunnel that Tyrell calculated must be directly over the hydroponic garden. A stiff, clammy breeze blew in their faces as they walked. At the far end, the tunnel ended in a vertical shaft.

"This is an old airshaft," she said. "It was part of the ventilation system before C.S. rebuilt the base for convection." She gestured up. "Look." She pointed the greenish beam upward, following the cable.

The shaft was six meters across. Above them, Lewis could see a huge, multibladed fan that completely filled the tunnel. Its blades were wind-milling slowly in the steady downdraft from Upside. The cable ran into the fan's motor housing.

"You're using the motor as a generator!"

"Yes. I've got three more fans higher up the shaft as well."

"Ingenious."

"Thank you." She smiled and looked pleased with herself. "It also serves to collect water. I closed off part of one of Corrective Service's ventshafts to increase the airflow through here. The condensate drips down the shaft walls and into my collecting pool." She pointed down through the hole in the floor with the flash. Water glinted below. "That's where I found you. The water gets siphoned down one more level to the garden. I just valve in as much as I need. The air goes on down the passage you came in through and back to the main ventshaft."

He looked at her with something close to awe. She made it sound so easy, and yet she must have started with nothing, working alone in the icy darkness with only her mind and the resources she managed to stumble across. He knew first-hand how quickly death could come in the mining tunnels.

They settled down to a routine. She taught him how to run the tiny ecosystem she'd set up.

It wasn't demanding and they had lots of time to talk. She was hungry for human contact, a hunger she had denied for a long time. For the most part, Lewis talked and she was content to listen while she rediscovered the habit of conversation. After a while, their roles changed and she talked more. They grew comfortable with each other, but even so there was a certain formality that served to keep them apart. She was aware of him as a man, he could tell that, but her body language told him to keep his distance. He respected that. She was rewarding in other ways. For the first time since he'd been captured at Terradyne's research base, he didn't feel the driving need to escape—from Camp 14, from society, from Mare Stellatis, from *himself*. It was a feeling so alien that at first he thought there was something wrong, but when he grew accustomed to it he found it was good.

He'd been there a month when she came to him, looking serious.

"We have a problem, Lewis."

He sat down on the floor. "What is it?"

"My resources are strictly limited by my available power. Almost all of it goes into the suntubes. My hydroponics garden will only yield so much. I increased the plant density as much as I could when you arrived and now we're getting the results of that, but we're still eating my reserves. There isn't enough for us both."

"Meaning?"

"Right now there's a lot in storage. We're slowly working our way into that. We're living on borrowed time, unless we can increase our energy input. I've been trying to think of a way to do that and I can't."

"What's the alternative?"

Her face was set. "One of us will have to leave."

"Meaning me."

"You're stronger than me. You're a trained killer." Her voice was flat and she avoided his gaze as she said it.

"You saved my life."

"You came to kill me once before." She was still staring off to the side.

Is she asking me to kill her? he wondered. "I need to wash the blood from my hands as well. There is another way."

She looked up. "What?"

"We can escape."

She laughed bitterly. "Nobody escapes from Mare Stellatis."

"I know how we can."

Despite herself she was interested. "How?"

"What you've done here proves that the maint stations weren't all stripped. I saw a map, there's some on the surface. Vehicle hangers. There could be pressure suits, tanks, and transport. We could make it to Farside Colony."

"And what then? Knock on the airlock door and say 'Excuse us, we're from Mare Stellatis. Please could we come in?'"

"We'll get in. They know no one gets out of here. They won't be expecting us."

"And then what? We won't last long at Farside. We'll be caught for sure. And there are worse things than Mare Stellatis."

"We won't stay long enough to get caught. We go to one of the colonies. They won't care where we're from. They'll take any warm body that shows up."

She looked at him closely. "You really think we'll find vehicles?"

He returned her gaze. "I think there's a good chance. I can't stop trying until I get out of here." *Or die in the attempt.*

"And if I don't want to come?"

"I'll go myself. I won't force you or try to stay."

"It would be suicide without my help."

"You're serving your penance by denying yourself freedom. I'm serving mine by trying to gain it. I can't give up."

"I'll come with you."

"Why?"

"You said it yourself. I can't bring back the dead. Penance is supposed to end with redemption. I've done my penance. Now I have to earn my redemption. Maybe helping you is it."

"All right." He paused. "Let's get going."

It was a simple plan. Jania knew which way to go to reach the crater wall. The vehicle hangers were at the ends of the longest surface tunnels, spaced beneath the crater rim. They would search the tunnels systematically in that direction, blazing their trail and heading to the lunar west and up at every opportunity. If they hit a dead-end, they would backtrack. She had sprayfoam and square meters of heavy synthetic fabric, stockpiled for some unknown purpose at one of the maint stations she'd stripped. They made loose garments from the fabric and insulated them with crumbled sprayfoam. They were cumbersome, but they would serve as protection against the bitter cold in the outer tunnels far from the convection system. Wire cable and poles would serve to cross any vertical shafts they came to; improvised shovels and picks would deal with rockfalls. It took a week to finish their preparations, and then they began.

At first they worked enthusiastically. Jania knew the tunnel system for a kilometer or more around her nest. From that starting point they started mapping westward. In the back of his mind, Tyrell knew that they were only just beginning. Even if they found a vehicle hanger and it wasn't stripped bare, they faced the possibility of a hundred-kilometer journey over the lunar surface, using equipment that had been abandoned ten years ago. Arriving at Farside Colony presented a whole new set of problems they couldn't even begin to address. Looked at in that light, the prospects for a successful escape seemed vanishingly small at best. Tyrell didn't allow himself to look at it in that light. Escape was the only option open to him, no matter what the odds. He didn't know what kept Jania going. She attacked the problems with the same energy and tenacity he figured must have allowed her to survive and build her sublunar nest in the first place

Days dragged into weeks and their map steadily expanded. They averaged better than twenty mapped kilometers a day and discovered several unstripped maint stations that gave them both hope and new resources. However, their explorations in the frigid reaches of the tunnel system increased their caloric output considerably and Jania's hoarded food reserves began to dwindle. They increased the plant density in the garden, but found it added only minimally to the yield. There was only so much energy available from the suntubes. They exercised their only other option and cut their rations to the bone. Both began to lose weight. Hope slowly became desperation as tunnel after tunnel dead-ended.

One day they were organizing themselves for another expedition when Jania dropped her pack. "We can't go on like this."

Lewis looked up, surprised. The comment was unlike her. "What option do we have?" he asked.

"We can use our brains, that's what we can do. Let's just stop a moment and think."

He put down his pack and sat on it, waiting.

She continued. "We aren't making progress fast enough. We're burning more energy than we get. We're going to starve before we get out at this rate."

"So what can we do about it?"

"There are three options." She ticked them off on her fingers as she listed them. "We can arrange to get more energy. We can try to get more food out of the energy we have. And we can use food we have more efficiently."

He nodded. "Fair enough. How do we implement them?"

"We can't implement them all. We can't get more power out of the fans than we already are."

"Perhaps we can get more fans. There's got to be more. This is a huge installation. It took more than that single shaft to ventilate it."

"Yes, but where are they? We've found lots of old shafts. How many have we found with fans? None. We can't afford to switch our search—too much of a gamble. And we can't increase the efficiency of the garden much above what it is now. We simply get more but smaller plants. However, we *can* use what we've got more efficiently."

"We're already on starvation rations." The thought reminded him of the pang in his stomach.

"That's not what I mean. Every step we take costs energy. We have to search efficiently. Right now it takes us most of a day just to walk out to the edge of our map. Then we survey a few kilometers of tunnel and come back. We need to get out there and set up a base camp."

He pondered for a second. "Save hiking and time as well, but we'll need an insulated tent or something or we'll lose the calories to the cold anyway."

She smiled. "So let's get to work on it."

The started to work on an extended equipment list, one that would allow them to make a week-long expedition. The biggest item was the insulated tent, made by the same procedure they'd used to make their insulated outerwear. Strapped to that were large fused stone jugs of water. Weight wasn't a problem—but bulk was. Their packs became awkward and balanced poorly. They also had to bring along containers to haul back waste. Everything had to be recycled through the hydroponics garden. They packed food for a week, and even with their reduced rations that put a sizable dent into their food reserves. There was tension in the air, desperation making them work with a sense of urgency. They worked long hours, knowing they were working against the clock. That in turn gave rise to fatigue that fed on the hunger they both felt. When they finally turned in it was to a deep, exhausted sleep and when they awoke it was with weary reluctance. It took them two days to assemble their gear. When it was ready, they struck out.

They made their way to the edge of their map, landmarked by a stripped maintenance station. They pitched their tent there and started off, systematically surveying the tunnels and blazing their trail. Fatigued as they were, the time dragged on. They brought Jania's clock with them to divide their time into regular periods of sleep and wakefulness, but without the suntubes to reset their circadian rhythms time soon lost meaning. Lewis found the experience akin to Downside ice mining—the darkness, fatigue, and hunger conspiring to narrow his world to the immediate moment and surroundings. It was hard to remain focused on their goals. There was one essential difference.

In Downside, he had only to meet the ice quotas to get food. Here there was no such guarantee. The knowledge provided an impetus that drove them on. There would be a very limited number of such expeditions. If they didn't find a surface exit soon they would starve.

When they slept, they slept together to conserve body heat. Unlike his experience in Downside he found himself intensely aware of Jania's femaleness beside him in the dark. There was comfort in the contact, and some frustration as well. He could sense that she too was aware of the sexuality inherent in the situation, but there was still a distance between them that neither seemed able to bridge. For the first time he had to admit to himself that he put up part of the barrier himself. *It's easier to trust her with my life than my feelings*, he reflected. Why hadn't it been like that with Cynthia? He understood the difference. He had allowed Cynthia to get close because even there he could keep her at a distance. With Jania, he knew that there would be no distance. Once the barrier was down it would be gone. There would be no middle ground. Neither could spare the time or energy such a change in their relationship would require. And even if the circumstances were different, he realized, neither was ready to accept such a change.

After six days they hadn't found a vehicle hanger. They had to return to the nest to reprovision and tend the hydroponic garden. Leaving it for a week was a risk—if a problem developed with a suntube or the water circulation they might come back to find it dead, and with it any hope of escape—or survival. Her concern was infectious and when they got back the first thing they did was check to make sure that it was running properly. Lewis breathed an audible sigh of relief.

They slept together in her bed that night, although in the warmth of the nest they didn't need to. There was an intimacy developing between them, expressed in touch and glance but never in words. The wall was starting to dissolve under the pressure of their situation and their mutual needs. As he held her in the dark Lewis wondered if they would live to see the tension resolved.

The spent only one day in the nest, long enough to give their circadian clocks a jolt, tend the garden, and replenish their supplies. Then they set out to extend their maps once again. They had found a promising tunnel, wide and straight. It had a railed walkway against the wall and long-dead lights set in the ceiling at regular intervals. Humans as well as machines had once used it. The very least they could expect to find was a maint station.

For the next week they trekked the length of

the tunnel, mapping the side passages that joined it like tributaries. They found the expected maint station on the second day, stripped to the walls. That was the first disappointment. By the fifth day they were tired and discouraged.

On the sixth day they found the hanger.

They were actually in the maint station before they knew they'd found more than a volcanic bubble. It was only when the tritium flash illuminated the huge pressure doors that they realized where they were. Beyond the pressure doors, there was a glassed-in control booth with its own airlock, and beyond that a vehicle, a heavy-duty cargo crawler like a ten-meter medicine capsule perched on six improbably large wire tires.

Their enthusiasm was short lived. When they got into the crawler, they found it stripped. The battery compartments over its three axles were open and empty. The control cabin had been gutted and the pressure gauges for the oxygen tanks stood at zero.

"Not exactly in pristine condition, is it?" he asked her.

Jania laughed. "You didn't expect to find it all juiced up and ready to go, did you?"

"No, of course not."

"Take inventory. It's got solar panels, so if we run in lunar day we won't need the batteries. We can bypass their circuit. How far is it to Farside?"

"A couple hundred kilometers or so, I'm not really sure."

"Well there's got to be a service road from there to here. If we can average twenty-five kliks an hour on it, that's only eight hours from here to Farside. That's not so much oxygen that we can't jury-rig something. We can do the same for the motor controls. We can do it."

"You're right. Let's find out what else we've got in here." They clambered down from the crawler and continued to explore the hanger. Tyrell was rummaging through empty tool lockers when he heard her scream. "God *damn* it!" He ran over and found her by the airlock doors, cursing in frustration.

"What is it?"

"Look. God damn it, *look!*"

He followed her finger. Around the seal where the airlock door met the frame was a continuous bead of metal. The lock had been welded shut. Slowly, deliberately, he pounded his fist against the steel, heedless of the pain.

She was shuddering, holding back tears. "We were so *close.*" He turned and took her in his arms and held her, and found his own tears welling up in response. *It's only a setback*, he told himself, and somehow holding her eased the disappointment.

On the way back, they told each other it was actually a breakthrough. The hanger had yielded valuable tools, including the mapcube from the crawler's control cabin. That alone would save them weeks of aimless exploration searching for other maint stations. More important, they had proven that the surface maint stations really existed, that they did house vehicles, and that it might be possible to solve the problem of getting one to run as far as Farside. Unspoken was the knowledge that if one hanger had its airlock welded shut, it was likely that they all did. They discussed ways of breaking the welds—with an improvised arc welder, with homemade thermite, with acid. None of the schemes was truly practical, but neither wanted to admit defeat.

Nevertheless, when they got back to the nest they took a break from exploration. Lewis spent a day hooking up a power connector to run the mapcube. Jania speculated on ways to get more power out of their generators. They were on the last of her food reserves. If they couldn't increase food output they'd be in trouble soon. Even without the weld problem it would take at least a month to get the crawler fixed up well enough to hazard the journey to Farside, assuming nothing went wrong. Their margin was too thin for error.

That evening, Lewis got the mapcube running and they studied it and compared it to their own maps. There were several surface maint stations that looked like good bets, as well as some underground ones they hadn't located that could yield equipment and supplies. They were planning the most efficient exploration path when inspiration struck Lewis.

"The water pipeline!"

"What about it?" Jania snapped. She had been tracing an ore tunnel through the tangled maze and he'd made her lose her place.

"That's the way out of here."

She looked at him. "You're out of your mind. First of all, we don't have access to Upside." She ticked off points on her fingers. "Second, we'd drown. Third of all, it doesn't lead to a pretty waterfall, it leads to the Farside refinery. If we somehow got through we'd wind up fractionated for deuterium."

"No, no, not that water pipeline. The old one."

"What are you talking about?"

"Look. Mare Stellatis used to supply deuterium for the whole fleet. There were hundreds of mining machines down in these tunnels digging up ice-ore by the cubic kilometer. The Downsiders can't hope to match their output. Corrective Services knows that. Farside Colony doesn't even need our water, they've got productive mines with real machinery that outproduce Mare Stellatis by a thousand to one. The only reason there even is a pipeline is to fulfill the Social Charter requirement that rehab colonies operate as functional economic units."

"So?" She pursed her lips doubtfully. "This isn't news."

"No! But think of it. All our water is shipped through a pipe half a meter in diameter. That would never have swallowed the output the base put out during the war."

"So they had a bigger pipe."

"A *much* bigger pipe. Empty now, of course, but it goes all the way through to Farside. It goes underground because if it were on the surface it would freeze at night and boil in the daytime. And it's right here. He stabbed the map with his finger."

"The Watercave!"

"Exactly. The Garden cavern used to be a water storage tank. The Watercave was the pipe head, or maybe they had an extension flume to take the pipeline down to the floor of the tank.

Corrective Services backfilled the tunnel and redid Mare Stellatis to make it a self-contained ecology. Air is heated by the suntubes in the garden, rises through upside and cools, then comes back through Downside. The Downsiders dump their ore down the ventshaft and the return air percolates through it and melts out the water. Water and air both come back to the Garden through the waterfall. That's the ventshaft closest to the Watercave. The others aren't full of mining spoil. They'd give access to the original pipeline."

She caught his enthusiasm. "So if we can get to it we could walk right through to Farside."

"It might be sealed," he cautioned. "It might be full of so much rock that we'll never get through. But we've got the rest of our lives to try."

"That tunnel is two hundred kilometers long at least. We'll be in it for days. It'll be cold. We'll need provisions."

"And climbing equipment to get down the ventshaft. That crawler had a winch on the front. How deep are the shafts?"

"They're at least the height of the Garden, that's a kilometer. Maybe more."

"What are we waiting for? Let's go."

They couldn't leave at once, of course. Getting back to the vehicle hanger to get the winch cable would be another overnight expedition. Since they where going to be there anyway, they might as well take advantage of the situation and explore some of the other vehicle hangers—finding them would no longer be a problem now that they had the mapcube. That in turn meant copying out the three-dimensional map, since they had no portable source of electricity to power it in the tunnels. And *that* meant finding some usable substitute for paper, since they had none. Eventually they settled on strips of orange fibron sheeting marked with beet juice. In addition, there were all the normal preparations for an expedition to be made. It was three days before they were ready to go back to the hanger.

They made use of the time to reconnoiter the ventshafts. There were five of them in a rough semicircle. They didn't appear in the mapcube, of course; they'd been added after the map was made. On their own maps, Jania labeled them R1 through R5. Tunnels intersected them at various heights. Twice they walked to each shaft, and the second time Lewis rappelled in a ways to see what the climbing would be like. R1 was out of the question, it was the one the Downsiders dumped their ice-ore down. They checked it out anyway, just to be thorough, and a shiver ran through Lewis's back as they peered over the brink. From far above he could hear voices, and his imagination made them sound like Checker and Myzer. It was even possible his imagination was right.

They finally settled on shaft R4. It had the lowest tunnel intersection, cutting a hundred meters off the thousand-meter climb, and unlike the others it was stepped, with small ledges every fifty meters that would aid their descent. It also had a pair of fifteen-centimeter conduits running up and down its length, leftovers from some stage of its construction, that would provide handholds and tie-off points. At least that's how it was for the first hundred meters. That was as far as Lewis could rappel with the cable Jania had on hand. They were tempted to try the descent right away—it would have been possible using the ledges as stopping points. Ultimately, they decided it was too risky. Once down the shaft they were committed, it would be impossible to come back up. If the old pipeline was blocked off or they ran into a snag they would be trapped.

When their supplies and equipment were ready, they headed back down the freezing outer tunnels to the vehicle hanger. They carried with them the last of Jania's food reserves. When they came back they would be completely dependent on fresh production from the hydroponics garden.

They reached the vehicle hanger in good time. The cargo crawler's winch drum yielded five hundred meters of woven carbon cable. Aided by their maps, they explored four other vehicle hangers the next day. One of them held another cargo crawler that gave them another five-hundred-meter cable. By their best estimates, that was enough. They made a cursory search of the hangers, more from habit than anything else, but rather than carry the equipment they found back they just listed it on the back of their map sheets. If they ever needed to come back for it, it would be there waiting for them. They didn't intend to need it. All the hangers had their airlocks welded shut. That was no more than they'd expected. The pipeline was a better bet anyway, if they could get to it, as it would keep them off the hostile lunar surface.

On the third day, they went back with their spoils, spirits high. They spent another full day readying packs and supplies for a two hundred-kilometer trek, executed in four fifty-kilometer stages. Theoretically, they should have been able to do a hundred kilometers in a single day under lunar gravity, but their experience hiking the mining tunnels had taught them that twenty-five kilometers was a more reasonable goal. Mare Stellatis was full of obstacles that slowed progress—sometimes to a literal crawl—as they squeezed past abandoned equipment, rockfalls, and spoil mounds.

Finally they were ready. Before they left, they

had a feast, gorging themselves on fresh fruit and vegetables. They had packed ample rations and the feast nearly stripped the garden bare. They were committed. If they didn't find a way out of Mare Stellatis, there was nothing for them but slow starvation. When they left, Jania took a last, long look around. Tyrell left her alone with her thoughts and waited down the tunnel for her to finish. *She built this with her blood and sweat. She put her heart into it, and now she'll never see it again.* For the first time, he realized just how much trust she was putting in him, to see her safely to freedom. The responsibility was sobering.

They hiked quickly to ventshaft R4. Once there, they drove a pair of meter-long steel reinforcing rods into the tunnel floor fifty meters from the shaft, then tied the ends of the cable to it. It was overkill—the cable and the rods would have supported ten times their weight, even on Earth, but as Tyrell pointed out, it didn't hurt to be sure. Jania had improvised two rappelling harnesses. They tied a rock to the end of the combined cables and let it snake over the edge, shaking it when it went slack to get it past the ledges. Then they shouldered their packs, clipped their harnesses to the cable, and went over. They took it easy, picking their way down by the glow of the tritium light. They could have gone much faster, but their packs made them awkward and there was no room for error. They leapfrogged at every ledge; the first person down tied off to one of the conduits, disconnected from the cable and held it steady for the one following.

Despite their caution, they made rapid progress. Jania had leapfrogged past Lewis when he felt the line go slack.

"Hey!" she called up. "I'm on the bottom!"

"What can you see?"

"There's a tunnel. I can see the pipeline from the lake leading away down it. And heavy power lines running into the conduits."

"Don't touch the cables!"

She laughed. "I'm not that eager for release."

"What else is there?"

"Just a second, I'm walking down to see."

He waited while minutes ticked by like hours. Finally her voice came back up the shaft.

"The tunnel is blocked by some kind of foamed sealant, heavier than sprayfoam. I think we can dig through it if it isn't too thick."

"Yes!" He threw up his arms in exultation.

"Why so pleased?" she called back. "I said it was blocked. We don't know what's behind the block."

"It isn't blocked, it's sealed. It's an airseal. The only reason for a seal there is to isolate the Farside

Colony air system from the one at Mare Stellatis. That means there's a passage right through to Farside. We're out of here!"

"Not yet, we're not. Let's find out just how thoroughly they closed us off."

"I'm coming down." Without waiting for her reply, he reconnected to the cable and slid down. He found her working on the airseal, digging at it with a knife from her backpack. She turned around when she saw him.

"This is it for sure, look." She swung her flash, revealing a half-meter pipe that ran down the side of the tunnel and into the airseal. "That must be the pipeline into the lake. Those conduits must carry the power for Upside."

"It looks right. How are you making out?"

"This is going to be hard work," she said. Her breath misted in the chill air. She hacked at the airseal again. The foam was tough and resilient, making it hard to cut, but she managed to tear away a fist-sized chunk.

"Maybe there's a better way."

"The best way is not to be here in the first place." She smiled wryly.

"You're right about that." He dug a prybar out of his pack and swung at the airseal with it. The foam yielded reluctantly. He found he could dig the chisel end into the foam but that the substance yielded like rubber when he applied leverage and the prybar slipped out. He couldn't cut any of it loose.

Jania stood back, pursing her lips as he tried again. "What if it's vacuum on the other side."

"We'll just pray there's more air in Mare Stellatis than there is vacuum in the pipeline."

"Let's hope it doesn't connect to the surface then."

"Amen to that." He swung the prybar again with no better results than before.

"Look, try this." She slipped her knife into one of the holes he'd made and sawed it back and forth. "Now pry the edges apart so I can work."

He did as she asked and she twisted the knife to cut into the airseal at an angle. As she extended the cut, he moved the prybar to peel the foam back and out of her way. She worked in a circle and soon they had a half-meter chunk of the stuff cut loose.

"I hope this thing isn't too thick," she said.

"Just keep cutting."

In the end they had to dig their way through three meters of airseal. The cut-and-pry method was so much more effective than anything else they tried that it was easier to cut large chunks free to provide enough room for them both to work standing up, even though they had to remove six times as much material as they would have if they'd simply dug a crawlway. It was slow, arduous work.

Lewis was cutting while Jania peeled the foam away when they broke through. Without warning the chunk they were working on *popped* free and was sucked into the darkness beyond. Air howled through a ragged half-meter opening.

"Vacuum!" yelled Jania. "Plug it, fast!"

Lewis grabbed a discarded slab of sprayfoam from the ground and pressed it against the opening. It held for a second, air hissing around its edges, and then it too was sucked out. He fell forward and was nearly pulled after it.

"Get something bigger!" She was already coming forward with a larger chunk. Together they slapped it over the hole. It was in no danger of being pulled through but it fit poorly and the atmosphere continued to roar through the gaps around the edges.

"We need more. We have to make it airtight," she said.

"How?"

"Grab more foam. The pressure will hold it on. We'll work out something better later." She was already moving down the tunnel, tossing scraps of foam to him. He took them and wedged them into the gaps. The roar diminished to a whistle, then burst out again as a new chunk dislodged an old one—which was promptly sucked into the void, taking several others with it.

"Dammit!" he howled, struggling with the foam. Several more chunks disappeared into the darkness.

"Here, use bigger pieces." She threw one to him. "We'll fill the whole tunnel back in—that'll slow it down, at least."

They went to work with a will, throwing chunks of foam haphazardly into the gap. As they worked, the roar became a whistle again. When they were through, the tunnel they had dug was full of foam chunks but air was still rushing through the gaps.

Jania stopped, hands full of pieces of foam. "How are we going to seal it?"

"I don't know. You have those tanks of spray-foam back at the nest. We'll have to climb back up and get some."

"That'll take too much time. We'll be out of air before we get back."

"We have to try. Let's go." Lewis turned to run back to the ventshaft.

Jania moved to follow, then held up a hand "No, wait, listen." She cupped an ear to the whistle. "It's slowing down. It's slowing down!"

Lewis imitated her. "You're right. Why?"

"Two possibilities. Either by some miracle

that mess is becoming an airseal again, or it's not a vacuum on the other side. Just a pressure differential."

"Pressure differential?" he said, not quite comprehending.

"Of course. Why didn't I think of it before? There are all sorts of reasons why the pressure would be different on the other side. Temperature's the biggest. We've just equalized the two sides."

"Are you sure?"

"Listen. It's slowing down. If we managed to plug the leak somehow, it would just stop."

"One way to find out." He started pulling away the foam they'd thrown in to block the gap. "If it starts again, close it up quickly and run for the sprayfoam."

She nodded. "Agreed."

Gingerly they removed chunk after chunk. The wind didn't suddenly pick up speed again. When they got back to the far side of the hole, the air was blowing past in a strong, steady breeze rather than the hurricane it had been when they first opened it. They shone the tritium flash through and saw a continuation of the tunnel they were in.

Jania sagged against the wall, limbs trembling with reaction. After a moment she started laughing. "We're *out*. We are out!" She pitched a hunk of foam at Lewis. After a second he slung one back and they spent a cathartic mad minute screaming and throwing foam at each other. He hugged her impulsively and kissed her out of sheer joy. She returned it enthusiastically and the kiss suddenly became intensely, passionately sexual. He pulled her close, feeling her breasts against his chest through the awkward thickness of their insulation suits. She tore impatiently at the closures, and he helped her with trembling fingers, stopping only to kiss her again and again. When the fabric came free they slid to the floor, heedless of the cold and the foam fragments.

He wasn't sure what stopped them. A threshold was crossed. The passion didn't go away, but the urgency did. They both wanted the wall to come down but neither was quite ready. They slowed their caresses, replacing desire with affection. After that they simply held each other for a long time, not talking. Eventually they set up the tent, through a mutual, unspoken agreement that they had come far enough that day. In bed they cuddled, gaining strength from each other as well as warmth. *The wall is already down*, thought Lewis. *Neither of us wants to admit it.* He caressed her hair as she slept, amazed at the joy the simple intimacy brought him.

When they woke up they set off, neither speaking about the change in their relationship. After a while, it was as if the incident had never happened. As if to make up for the difficulty of breaching the airseal, the tunnel was easy traveling, with no rockfalls or other obstacles to slow them down. The tunnel was a natural lava tube, bored out in places to widen it. They made good time, and Tyrell estimated that if nothing slowed them down they should make Farside the next day. Nothing did slow them down, but eventually they tired before they reached their goal and pitched camp again. Secretly, Tyrell wondered if Farside was much farther. The two hundred-kilometer distance they'd been working with was just a round-figures estimate. Neither of them had expected to be consigned to Mare Stellatis and so neither had bothered to learn anything about it beyond what was common public knowledge. If they didn't reach the other end of the tunnel by the end of tomorrow's march they would be in trouble. Their bridges were burned; there was nothing to do but press on to the end of their supplies and hope they made it. Tyrell was confident he could go two or three days without food, but water was another matter. It was ironic that there was a whole pipeline full of it right beside them, so close and so far out of reach. Eventually he put the problem out of his head. He would worry about it when he had to, not before.

Two days later, they were both worrying about it. Their food and water were gone and the tunnel showed no sign of ending. He had no way of knowing how far they'd gone or how far they had yet to go. There was no point in turning back, they had to keep going no matter what. That night they talked about it, but there was nothing to do but keep going as long as they could. Tyrell hammered impotently on the water pipeline with the prybar, hoping to somehow puncture it and gain access to the vital fluid, but the steel remained undented.

They set out the next day and marched in grim silence, dizzy with hunger and thirst. They were fatigued and their pace slowed. They had today and perhaps tomorrow, and then one of them would collapse. The end for them both wouldn't be long after. Starvation and thirst weren't pleasant ways to die. He'd lost track of how long they'd marched that day. Far enough; soon they would have to stop for the night.

Jania saw it first and yelled. Tyrell caught up to her. It was another pressure seal. The pipeline drove right through it. They were too exhausted to rejoice. Patiently they began to dig at the tough, resilient material. Progress was as slow and frustrating as it had been in the Watercave, but now they knew their goal must be near. The vibration of heavy machinery came clearly through the floor, it could only be the deuterium refinery. The nearness of freedom drove them on. The possibility that the other side might yet be in vacuum didn't even occur to them.

After several hours they broke through. Cold air howled past them into the space beyond the seal. They were looking into another bubble cavern, perhaps two kilometers across and half as high. Their vantage point was halfway up one wall. Laid out on the floor like a child's construction set was Farside Colony's deuterium refining plant. The pipeline from Mare Stellatis snaked down the side of the bubble to join a spaghetti tangle of other pipes that fed a series of ranked storage bubbles. Fractionating towers and other less identifiable structures crowded the floor of the cavern. Workers moved about the massive complex like insects. The steady rumble of heavy machinery filled the air and penetrated the rock.

A sense of exhilaration swept over Lewis. Jania hugged him spontaneously. "We did it!"

Lewis pursed his lips. "Now comes the tricky part. We'll need clothing, money, and idents." His serious words didn't detract from the euphoria of freedom.

Jania smiled almost smugly. "Wrong, we just

need money. That'll take care of the rest. And I've already taken care of the money."

"How?"

She grinned and pulled a cashwafer out of her pocket. "I found a body a long time ago. A miner who got lost when they shut the base down, I think. The body went into the hydroponics and I kept the rest. I brought this along just in case we made it."

He took it from her and examined it. Darkened areas on its surface defined a number—4906, followed by the Lcr symbol of lunar currency.

"How much can we buy with that?"

"I don't know what lüns are worth, but it's a start."

He looked at her with only half-pretended adoration. "You're amazing."

She smiled with half-pretended modesty. "I know."

"Let's get going, it's going to be a long climb."

"Where do we go when we get to the bottom?"

He pointed across the cavern to a building set against the far wall. "That looks like the administration block. There'll probably be access to the rest of the colony through it. If not, we'll just circle around the edge until we find something."

"Sounds good." She swung her legs over the edge. "Let's go."

They started down, using the support brackets on the pipe for handholds. It was nerve wracking even in the low gravity. The brackets were two meters apart, which meant it was impossible to climb them like a ladder. Instead they had to wedge their hands awkwardly between the rock wall and the curve of the pipe, lowering themselves until they could grab the next bracket. A single slip would be fatal. Tyrell wished they'd been able to bring the cables they'd used to descend the ventshaft.

Eventually they reached the bottom, intact and, so far as they could tell, undetected. They moved toward the administration structure, trying as much as possible to keep out of sight of the catwalks and look inconspicuous at the same time. Occasionally they saw workers dressed in bright orange or yellow jumpsuits. However, nobody interfered or even seemed to notice them. Neither talked, although talking might have broken the tension. At last they reached the base of the administration building. Unlike most of the structures in the refinery cavern, it was a separate air containment region, with access over catwalks leading through irising pressure seals.

"Hey, look what I've got." Tyrell was examining a bright yellow box labeled EMERGENCY mounted on a prominent pole by the catwalk stairs.

"What is it?"

He opened the box. "Stretch suits." He pulled out a pair of form-fitting one-piece garments, each bright yellow. "Now we can go in style."

Jania regarded the suits dubiously. They were one-size-fits-all, designed to prevent decompression long enough to get the wearer out of an emergency. "Do you think that's wise?"

"They'll be less conspicuous than what we're wearing now. Come on." He started taking off his clothes.

"I suppose you're right." She started changing as well.

She was done before he was and urged him on. "No use waiting. Let's do it."

"We'll go in through the top entrance. They'll be less likely to stop us going down than up."

She nodded. They climbed the stairs to the top catwalk and followed it into the administration structure, through an automatic pressure-lock. Everyone they saw was wearing the same style jumpsuit as the workers on the refinery floor, although there were more colors. Tyrell felt uncomfortably conspicuous, but their unusual attire attracted glances and nothing more. At that the stretch suits stood out less than their crude, bulky, and obviously improvised insulation garments would have. Three flights of stairs brought them to the main level and they found a corridor that led out of the complex and into the heart of Farside Colony. There was a thumbprint scanner and a security guard in the entrance lobby, but they were to control entry, not exit.

She grabbed his arm. "Look." He followed her gaze to a water fountain. They ran to it, the need to appear casual forgotten in their haste, and took turns slaking their thirst. When they were done the security guard was watching them, but didn't try to stop them as they left.

Lewis and Jania simply walked out the door and into the pedestrian arcade. It was an arched tunnel, fifteen meters across at floor level and lined with offices. People bustled along the walkways, and two large slidewalks down the center of the arcade carried people with distant destinations. Every fifty meters, a pair of trees planted in the floor flanked the slidewalks, growing toward the suntubes overhead. There was an omnipresent burble of conversation. Again, nobody interfered with them. Unlike the refinery employees, the crowd was sporting an amazing variety of clothing styles, ranging from the elaborate to the nearly nude.

They boarded the slidewalk to avoid blocking traffic and Jania looked around at the passing crowd. Nobody spared them as much as a second glance. "Maybe we don't need clothes after all." she said. "Let's find somewhere to sit and plan, but first we need food I'm awfully hungry."

"Agreed. Let's find a bank terminal and find out if this cashwafer still works."

"There's a mapboard over there." She pointed ahead of them. They got off the slidewalk and went over. The nearest bank terminal was just opposite them. They picked the first vacant screen and she fed the wafer into the machine, then punched the Add Value key. There was a tense moment while it processed the request. The card was old; it could be defective or obsolete.

The screen flashed, "Enter transfer account number."

Jania pushed CANCEL. The machine spat out the wafer and she took it. "We're flush."

"So how much is 4906 lüns worth anyway? Is it enough for a scriber? A room for the night? An aircar? A house?"

"They don't have houses here, remember? It's got to be enough for a meal, anyway. The prices on the menu will let us know just how rich we are.

"We just need enough for a colony ticket."

"Let's see if we have enough for lunch."

They rode the slidewalk until they spotted a quickfood outlet. There they feasted on breaded shrimp and vegetable soup with creamed papaya for desert. Neither said anything during the meal—both were too intent on eating. Afterward they paid with the cashwafer. The balance read 4848 Lcr. They waited until they were outside and beyond casual eavesdropping before they talked.

Tyrell started the conversation. "That was fifty-eight lunar credits including tax, just over one percent of our reserve. How many meals is a flight to ETS and a colony ticket?"

"I don't know. We aren't rich, but we have some breathing room. A ticket can't be so far out of reach"

"Let's find a travel agency."

"Better yet, let's find a phone."

There was one just outside the restaurant. Jania made the call while Tyrell stayed out of range of the vid pickup, watching the crowd for danger. *Soldier's reflex. Unnecessary now. Nobody even knows we've escaped.* Still, he kept watching. She punched some buttons on the phonedex, then slid the cashwafer through its reader slot and dialed. He could hear her talking to someone, then she punched the screen off and turned to him.

"Well?"

"Good news and bad news. The flight to Earth Transfer Station is seven hundred lüns each. The colony ticket is free with up to twenty kilograms carry-on baggage. It gets expensive for more mass but we don't have to worry about that."

"And the bad news?"

"We have to submit colonist applications. It's just a formality—they told me our acceptance is automatic since we're Line One citizens. They can process us on the spot and send us out today. Except we're not citizens. We need idents for the application and we haven't got them."

He considered. "We have cash. Maybe we can get around needing them."

She shook her head. "We need idents anyway. If we get caught without them, they'll do a retina scan. When they find out we don't exist they won't even call Corrective Services, they'll call the SIS. They won't send us to Mare Stellatis this time around. They'll space us on the spot." She shuddered. "At best."

"Well, we'll just have to find a way to get them."

"How?"

"I have an idea. Let's find a strip club."

"A what?"

"A strip club. Naked men and women dancing for an audience."

She rolled her eyes. "I know what a strip club

is. What do we want one for? I assume it's for more than entertainment."

"We need to find someone who can supply us with forged idents. We won't find anyone like that there, but we'll find somebody who knows how to find one."

"Good thinking."

As it turned out, it was simple. The phonedex yielded a tunnel address for a place called The Cat's Meow. They rode the slidewalk as far as they could, then had to walk. The bar was in one of the original sections of Farside, built before the slidewalks. The tunnels were narrower and there was a general air of decay. Once upon a time, this section of the colony had been the pride of the United Nations. Now it was the red light district. Several times they passed security officers, walking in pairs or riding airscooters. Each encounter raised their pulse rate as they walked past, pretending nonchalance. Even a routine inquiry would be disastrous. The patrols passed without paying them any heed and their pulse rates returned to normal. Until next time.

They didn't bother finding The Cat's Meow. The first establishment they came to was called Paradise Lost. It was garishly lit and pounding music thumped from the interior as naked holograms gyrated in the windows. The interior was dim, save for the spotlights on the stage, where a dancer was stripping to the beat. Inside a sunken transparent cube, a man and a woman were having sex to the cheers of the intoxicated crowd.

Tyrell made his way to the bar and waited for the harried bartender to make his way over to him.

"What're you having?"

"I'm looking for someone."

The bartender's expression froze. "I haven't seen him. If you're not buying, you'll have to leave. The show ain't free."

"I didn't say it was a him, and I am definitely buying. I'm looking for someone who can get things. If I find what I'm looking for it'll be well worth your while."

"How much?"

"A hundred lüns when I meet who I want, five hundred when I get what I'm looking for."

The bartender suddenly became friendly again. "Well, why didn't you say so? I'll see what I can do." The man moved away.

Lewis joined Jania at a table and watched the show, for want of anything better to do. A new dancer was on the stage, a petite, athletic blonde with talent beyond what the crowd could appreciate. She danced with an energy and enthusiasm that contrasted sharply with the previous stripper's bored lethargy. She had finished her set and was doing an encore when a man sat down at their table.

"Mac says you're looking for something." The stranger leaned back.

"That's right."

"Anything I can help you with?"

"Idents."

The man rubbed his chin. "Hmmmm, could be expensive. Could take some time too." He leaned forward. "You in trouble?"

Tyrell let himself look bored. "Not really."

"Mac tells me you don't have any cash."

Tyrell moved to show him the wafer, but Jania raised her hand to stop him. "We have cash," she said.

"Let's see it." He'd caught the interchange between them.

"Can you get us the idents?" Tyrell redirected the conversation.

"I already told you I could."

"No, you didn't. You just told me it could take time and money. I already knew that."

"Trust me, I can get them."

"How much?" Jania interjected.

The stranger leaned back again. Negotiations had begun. "That depends on how fast you need them."

Tyrell shrugged. "Longest time, lowest price."

"I don't believe you."

"You have idents, we have money. Maybe we can make a deal. You don't make them yourself. Maybe someone else knows your connection, too. I'm not in a hurry."

"Two thousand lüns each." The stranger smiled.

"Too high." *Always reject the first offer.*

It was the man's turn to shrug. "That's the price."

"One thousand."

The man raised his eyebrows. "You think you can get these anywhere?" He did his best to sound incredulous. "I'm talking quality product here."

Tyrell injected sarcasm into his voice. "I wouldn't be talking to you if I didn't know you were the best."

"Seventeen-fifty."

"Twelve hundred."

"Fifteen hundred."

"Thirteen hundred, take it or leave it." Tyrell folded his hands.

"Half up front." *Deal done.*

Jania held up her hand. "When we see that the idents are in the works."

"Sold."

Tyrell stood up. "Let's go then. What do I call you?"

"Salvin will do."

"A pleasure doing business with you, Salvin."
They maneuvered their way through the throng to
the exit.

Once they got outside, Tyrell paused. "Wait
for me here." He left Jania and Salvin and went
back inside to the bar. He beckoned Mac over with
the cashwafer. "Here, let me give you a tip." He
took the bartender's readerwand and ran it over
the wafer's charge target, then tapped it for a hundred lunar credits. "Salvin will settle the rest with
you when we're done," he lied. He turned to go,
then turned back and smiled. "And thanks."

Salvin led them through the tunnels of the red
light district. The atmosphere circulation was poor
and there was a sour smell in the air. Glowstrips
rather than suntubes provided the lighting, and
many of them were in need of replacement. The
narrow tunnels were full of human detritus, people
who for one reason or another had come to Farside
and for one reason or another were unable to leave.
Eventually, he led them through a pressure seal into
a residential corridor and down a dim hallway to a
nondescript door. He knocked on the door.

Tyrell was taken aback by the person who
answered the door. The man's face was young,
perhaps twenty, but his body was as wizened and
twisted as an old man. He sat in a powered air-

chair with his legs strapped to their supports. His hands were gnarled, their joints swollen, but his eyes were sharp and intelligent.

"Salvin, well, well. You got what you owe me?"

"I've got some business for you." Salvin's demeanor had changed, he sounded almost deferential.

"What kind of business?"

"Idents."

"How much?"

Salvin paused. Clearly he'd hoped to have this conversation in private. "Thirteen hundred. Each."

"That'll do. We'll knock your commission off your tab, shall we?"

"I need some now, Ace."

"You can have two hundred."

"I need more."

"You can have two hundred. Next time, don't bring customers to my door." The man in the air-chair turned his attention to Jania and Lewis. "You can give Salvin his two hundred now. Then come in and we'll see what we can do for you." He pressed the joystick on his chair, swiveling it around and going back into the apt without waiting for a response.

Tyrell pulled out the cashwafer. "You got a reader?"

Salvin produced his beltcomp and Tyrell ran the wafer past its window and tapped it for two hundred lüns. The wafer was down to 4545. Salvin snapped the beltcomp back into place. "Glad to be of service," he said, with an attempt at his former cockiness, then turned and walked back down the hallway. Jania and Lewis looked at each other, then went into the apt, closing the door behind them.

The apt was a mess. Nameless electronic components, many obviously handmade, were strewn on surfaces and piled on the floor. Journals were stacked and scattered on the floor, mixed with dirty clothing and empty quickfood containers. The place stank of sweat, ozone, and sundry less identifiable odors. Jania wrinkled her nose pointedly. Lewis followed the hum of the airchair's fans into a combination bedroom and office. The bed was unmade and the desk completely covered with a partially disassembled computer. The computer was on and running—surprising in view of the fact that half its components were hanging out of it, supported only by their connector cables. The man in the airchair was waiting for them.

"I'm Ace," he said, "As you might have gathered from our friend out there. I don't usually do this in person but I trust Salvin's judgment, more or less, when his neck is on the line. First you can give me twenty-four hundred creds, then you can tell me what I can do for you."

"We need idents," said Jania. Tyrell offered the cashwafer. "It was to be half up front."

Ace accepted the wafer. "I'll take it all, just to save hassle. As you can see—" he gestured down at his legs, "I'm not about to run out on you." He scanned the wafer and tapped it, holding it so they could see how much he was taking. He looked at Tyrell for verification and returned the wafer on his nod.

"Idents, yes, so I gathered. Anything special you need on them?"

"What can we get?"

"Anything you want, if you think you can make it stick. Police status, diplomatic status, corporate access. You name it, I'll do it." He ran his fingers over the computer keyboard like a maestro warming up for a concert.

"Normal citizen idents will be fine."

"Wise choice; why be greedy? Should have asked you before paying anyway—it's a value-added service. Names?"

"You can pick them."

"I like you, my friend, you let my creativity run free. All right, eyes and thumbs, please." Ace held up his scanwand. First Jania then Lewis bent over to have their retinas and thumbprints scanned. Ace punched some keys on his keyboard, watched as cryptic results flowed over the screen.

"OK, tapped. You guys got any legal problems?"

"No."

Ace raised an eyebrow. "Be straight, my friend—I'll know in a minute anyway."

"I don't think you'll find anything."

"Hmmm, we'll see," said Ace, not entirely convinced. His fingers danced over the keyboard. He paused as he examined the results, frowned and tapped in another series of commands. There was a long pause, then more data flowed over the screen. Ace pushed back his airchair and looked up at them.

"This is very interesting."

"What is?"

"You're right, I didn't find anything. Absolutely nothing, to be precise. You don't seem to exist on the moon. No legal, no medical, no admin, no birth, no death, no immi, no nothing. Lunar databanks don't record your thumbprints or your retinas. Period."

"We're from Earth."

"Is that so? Normally, everybody gets registered when they come in through customs. That's what the immi files are for. They just read the data off your ident, of course."

"Very odd indeed. They must have made an error."

"Odd is right. So odd that I actually went so far as to send a query to Earth, just in case you were from there. And guess what?"

"No result there, either?"

"Exactly."

"Well, we're a very unusual couple, but you already knew that. That's why we need the idents. We've paid and we expect you to deliver at that price."

"Oh no, you misunderstand. I'm not trying to put you to the strip. That's Salvin's job. I am talking about the technicalities of ident generation."

"Meaning what?"

"Listen, my friend. You can't just pop people into existence on the registration system. There are checks, verifications. With your retprints I can access your record, make changes, make you someone else. The system lets me do that because I have developed the necessary access. But if I create a new record, suddenly the checksums don't add up. Other ways to do it—sub your data into someone else's ident, dupe the card data. That works until the real person uses the ident the same time you do. Either way, they put the strip on the system until they find the problem. That means until they find *you*, and more importantly—*me*.

The key to this game is knowing how far to go and going no further than that."

"So what can you do for us?"

"How long do you need this ident for? Don't play games with me—I'm on your side."

"A day, maybe two."

"Getting out of town, eh? Colonies?" He paused. "Don't answer, doesn't matter. This has possibilities. Starting when?"

"As soon as possible."

"Well you're in luck, here's the deal. I can pull up the newsfiles. . . ." He tapped on the keyboard as he spoke and data flowed across the screen. "Scan the obits for a deader. . . ." He tapped some more. "Call up the medical files. . . ." More data, this time under a caduceus logo. "Download the eyecharts for the retpattern. . . ." He keyed a series of commands and the familiar blood vessel pattern of someone's eye appeared on the screen. "Access the deader's registration . . ." (more tapping) ". . . and sub in your data." He repeated the process, gnarled fingers flying too fast for Tyrell to follow the commands, then turned around looking pleased with himself. "Smile for the camera, friends." He pointed to the voxvid pickup on top of his screen. First Lewis and then Jania looked in it, while Ace froze their images into his system's memory. A few more keystrokes and he pushed his chair back.

"The deaders aren't going to be using their idents any time soon. It's Saturday; their certificates won't be processed till Monday; that's when the bells go off. Except they won't. Here's the deal. You do whatever you're going to do until eight-hundred Monday morning, Farside time. At that point, I'm switching the deader data back the way it was. No bells go off when the certificates get processed. Everything stays quiet. You got until then. Don't get caught."

"Thanks."

"Don't thank me, my friend, pay me a bonus. Five hundred lüns. I need hardware."

"It's yours," said Tyrell, thinking of Mac the bartender who would be expecting that much from Salvin. He handed over the cashwafer and watched while Ace tapped it for five hundred more credits. Then Ace tapped a key and two sheets of hardcopy slid out of his printer. Another key and a partially disassembled box beside the computer whirred to life. After a minute it spat out two ident cards, complete with security seals over their holograms. Ace handed the cards and hardcopies to Jania and smiled. "Got the sealer unit out of the registration office trash. Don't ask me where I got the ident blanks. Initiative, friends. Initiative and creativity. Damn few cops have either." He slid his airchair to the door and they followed. "Don't be stupid and you don't get caught."

"Thanks."

"It's my job. Good luck out there. Drop me a line from the colonies." He closed the door.

"Well, now we're set. Tickets, colony application, and we're out of here."

"So far so good. It's just about twenty-two. We've got thirty-four hours to get on a colony ship."

Jania was examining the hardcopies. "These are the background details for our idents." She scanned down the first page. Suddenly she chuckled.

"What is it?"

"The name." She checked the other sheet and laughed again. "Jane Seymour and Henry Tudor. Well, we knew he had a sense of humor."

"I don't get it, what's funny about those names?"

"Henry the Eighth, king of England in the first half of the fifteen hundreds and his third wife, Jane Seymour. Let's hope we don't get a colonization officer who's studied British history." She laughed again. "And no cutting off my head."

"I thought that was Anne Bolyne."

"I'm not taking any chances." She poked him in the ribs and laughed.

They walked back to the slidewalk in high spirits, then rode it to the travel agency Jania had called before, studying their backgrounds. When they got there, it was closed. Tyrell suppressed a surge of panic. They had a window of opportunity defined by the time their idents were valid and the total available on their cashwafer. When either ran out, they'd be fugitives in Farside's underworld. Sooner or later they'd be caught. Whatever forces in the government and SIS had moved to silence their knowledge of Hype in the first place would move again. This time, their sentence was unlikely to be as merciful as oblivion in Mare Stellatis.

They ran through the phonedex looking for an agency that was open all night and went there. The misstep cost them an hour and a half. Then they sweated through another two hours at the travel agency while their colony applications were completed and the travel arrangements booked. A single bureaucratic snag and their window would be gone. Their flight left at ten-hundred-thirty the next day and arrived at ETS at midnight Sunday. There they would transfer to CTS *Charity*, currently boarding for the Erebus colony. *Charity* would be boarding until late Monday and departure was scheduled for one hundred Tuesday morning. The process ground on, slowly but without problems. Their idents passed without question and their colony applications were approved as a matter of routine.

"I'm worried," Jania said when she saw the departure time. "Our idents are going to expire before we're out of the system."

"It won't matter. Once we're on *Charity*, nobody will care who we are. We've got eight hours to get through boarding control. In fact we've got eight hours to get *into* boarding control, because that's just as good as being on *Charity*. It's not a wide margin, but we'll be fine."

"It is what it is," she said, unconvinced. "What now?"

"Find a hotel and sleep. I'm exhausted. How much do we have left?"

"Enough that we don't have to sleep in the streets. Let's go."

They grabbed the first hotel they could find, checked in and collapsed. Lewis remembered to call the desk and set up a wakeup call. Missing the shuttle would be disastrous. There was only one bed and they shared it, too tired to do anything but appreciate the warmth. They fell into a deep, dreamless sleep, and morning came too early.

They breakfasted in the hotel's restaurant, then slidewalked to the port. Clearing customs was easy with no baggage. Once again, their idents passed without difficulty. They were early for the flight and there was a long and stressful wait in the passenger lobby. Jania bought a book and tried to read it. Lewis just watched the people going by, trying not to react to the alert security officers who patrolled up and down the departure section.

Finally their boarding call came. Almost limp with relief, they lined up to have their tickets checked by the gate agent. She didn't even glance at them, just waved her scanwand past. When it beeped she gave them a plastic smile. "Enjoy your flight," she said with near sincerity. Tyrell returned her smile as best he could. Once on board there was more waiting but less stress, then, finally, takeoff.

The takeoff was gentle, just half a G, but it was far heavier than the moon's pull and it was enough to make Tyrell uncomfortable. He looked at Jania, who didn't look happy. She had been a lunar resident much longer than he had. *I hope she can readapt to planetary gravity.* Erebus's pull was a respectable .8 G. He settled down as best he could to while away the long flight.

They were both asleep when the shuttle docked at ETS. They had a luxurious meal at an overpriced restaurant with windows cut in the floor, a meal that took up most of the balance on their cashwafer. When they were done, they reported to the colony registration desk. From there, everything changed. They were herded like cattle through a series of inoculations, medical exams, and bureaucratic hoops, acutely aware of the dwindling time left before their idents became invalid. Loading a colony transport took days, and there was always at least one at ETS being boarded. The system was designed to process people as efficiently as possible, but with little regard for their comfort. They had become nonpersons, and thus were beneath notice. In other circumstances, Lewis would have bridled at the treatment. This time he actually welcomed the anonymous indifference of the staff. Their time limit expired while they were going through the process, but after they cleared in nobody asked to see their idents. Significantly, most of the colonists going through the process with them were Line Two refugees. Tyrell wondered if the system would be so dehumanizing if most colonists were Line One citizens.

Hours later, they joined an endless line waiting to board the transfer pods to CTS *Charity*. Overhead, Tyrell could see the line of office windows on the terrace level over the passenger arcade. One of those windows was the one he'd looked out, plotting an escape that was finally going to happen. The line advanced in fits and starts as pods were loaded and cycled through the docking bays. They endured the wait stoically. Once aboard *Charity* they were free, that was what mattered.

There was a disturbance at the back of the line. "What's going on up there?" Jania asked. Tyrell leaned sideways to look up the line of people. His blood ran cold. A pair of ETS Security police were working their way down the colonists, checking paperwork and retprints with scan-wands.

"ETS Security, verifying the colonists."

"I didn't think they cared once you were through colony registration."

"They care about something this time," said Tyrell with an edge of bitterness.

"They're looking for a runner," reasoned Jania. "But it can't be us. They can't know we've escaped, much less that we're here."

"It's after eight-hundred; our idents won't pass. They might be looking for someone else—but they're going to catch us."

"It's only nine-hundred. If Ace swapped the idents back, the change probably hasn't been uploaded here yet."

"We can't count on that—we've got to dodge the check."

"How?"

Lewis pointed backward to a spot where the

cattle-run divider was broken. The opening was closed off with a semiornamental rope, nothing more. "Work our way back down the line and get over the divider when they aren't looking. Give them ten minutes progress here and then rejoin the line at the front. If anyone asks us, we're just lost."

"Good enough. Let's do it."

They pressed back through the throng, trying to do it inconspicuously. When they were beside the rope divider, Lewis looked at the faces around them. None were paying them any particular heed. He turned his attention to the security guards working their way down the line. Their attention was fully focused on their work.

"Now," he said. They stepped over the divider together. "Just keep walking. We'll find a washroom and hide for a few minutes." They moved away from the line of colonists.

"Excuse me!" The words were polite but the tone brooked no argument. They whirled around to see a pair of guards approaching them. "I'd like to see your idents." The female guard was holding up a scanwand, the male had his hand on his holster. It was clear they suspected something.

The tableau froze for a second, then Jania dodged and sprinted down the corridor. Tyrell cursed. *That's torn it.* One guard took off after her, yelling into her commlink. The other dropped to a crouch and drew his jetpistol. Tyrell lashed out with his foot and caught the guard on the wrist. The pistol sailed out of reach and the guard yelled in pain but rolled away from Tyrell's attack. Tyrell followed up, then backed off as the guard rolled to his feet and drew his stunwand.

"Halt!" The other guard had stopped running and drawn her jetpistol. "Halt or I'll shoot!"

Jania kept running, moving fast in the low gravity. A siren began wailing and the emergency pressure doors in the corridor in front of her began to iris shut. The guard facing Lewis took advantage of his distraction to bring the stunwand down. Tyrell caught the motion in the corner of his eye and automatically blocked the blow with his forearm, realizing too late that the instinctive response was the wrong one this time. The stunwand connected with a crack and Tyrell collapsed around an explosion of pain. His arm and shoulder went numb as he desperately dodged another swing of the stunwand. Jania was still running toward the closing iris. If she didn't make it through, she'd be cut in half. She ran faster in response, putting muscle into each long, gliding stride, aiming for the center of the iris. She was going to make it.

The guard with the jetpistol fired. Time contracted for Tyrell as Jania made the final leap that would carry her through the closing pressure seal. The tiny rocket seemed to crawl, overtaking her with painful slowness. The stunwand connected with Tyrell's ribcage and he convulsed again, blacking out for a split second. When his eyes opened the female guard had fired again, even as the first slug caught Jania in the lower back. Blood and bone fragments erupted from the impact point and her arms came up reflexively, as if she were imploring heaven for deliverance. The second slug hit her square between the shoulder blades, driving her forward and down. Her body cartwheeled to the floor, spraying blood. She slid into the bottom of the pressure seal. A moment later, the contracting iris shut with a dull *thud*. Lewis didn't hear it, nor did he hear the guard standing over him order him to his feet. His vision blurred and he saw Section Leader Valdi lying sprawled on the pavement of an Alliance research base. He called to her and she looked up, the front of her torn combat uniform soaked in blood. But her face was Jania's and she was telling him that she was dying. Somewhere someone was yelling but the noise was drowned out by a roaring in his ears. *We've come so far*, he thought, and then the roaring grew until the world went black.

CHAPTER FOUR

EXALTATION

EARTH TRANSFER STATION SECURITY never learned who he was. At first they thought they knew. Both his and Jania's idents and retina scans passed without incident. They suspected something, because Jania had run and because Line One citizens rarely went to the colonies without some compelling reason. Beyond that suspicion, their prisoner was just a line-jumper. They were eager to find something. They needed to transform Jania's death from police overreaction to the interception of a dangerous offender. Tyrell simply failed to respond to their questions. He sat on the bunk in his cell, bent forward with his head in his hands. *The ident passed. We didn't need to run. Now I've lost her.* And it was only then that he realized just how large a loss that was.

Two hours later, the security database computer at ETS flagged an error. It had two sets of data for one ident-record code. The second set had come up from Farside's databanks in the routine daily upload. One dataset corresponded to Farside citizen Henry Tudor, currently being held prisoner by ETS security. The other corresponded to Myslen Chandresahn, another Farside citizen who had died Friday evening at the colony hospital. ETS Security breathed a sigh of relief. They still didn't know who they were holding, but they knew they were off the hook for the shooting. Confidently they sent the retprints to Earth with a search request.

Their search returned blank, and they went to work on Tyrell with a vengeance, trying to pressure information out of him with alternating threats and promises. He failed to respond. On the third day the SIS arrived, although ETS hadn't contacted them. The SIS took over the prisoner and deleted the entire case file. ETS Security was told in no uncertain terms that the incident had never occurred. They were only too glad to agree. Case closed.

When the SIS took him, Lewis recognized the same gray man who had read the charges to him in the van the day he was arrested a lifetime ago. "I thought I'd never see you again, Lewis," he chided with mock concern. "You're going to wind up wishing you stayed in Mare Stellatis."

Tyrell ignored him, and no one else seemed

inclined to talk. They didn't even ask him questions; they didn't try to find out how he'd escaped.
They simply shackled him and locked him in a
room. The next day they put him on a fast courier
ship. Tyrell noticed the name on the airlock door as
they hustled him on board—HG492 *Quicksilver*. It
was the only detail that stood out in his memory
afterward. Nobody bothered to tell him what his
destination was. He didn't care enough to ask, or
even wonder. He found out by accident later.
Deneb Kaitos. The name meant nothing to him.

Quicksilver was eighteen days in transit. The
time passed with leaden slowness under her three-
G acceleration. He ate when he was fed, otherwise
he was indifferent to his fate. *I am resigned.* The
loss of Jania had burned the driving need to
escape out of him. He didn't even know they'd
arrived until the dropshuttle rendezvoused with
them and they put him aboard it. Through its windows, he could see a glaring white planet,
wrapped in layers of streaky clouds. It was almost
too bright to look at, so he didn't. Eventually they
grounded. The heavy gravity that pulled at Tyrell
was barely less than *Quicksilver*'s maximum acceleration. This wasn't a colony world, then; it was
some dense rockball on the rim of explored space.
Its atmosphere was clearly unbreathable—the
landing pad was an elevator that took them into

an underground shiplock. He overheard two of the crew talking about poisonous hydrocarbons under pressure and filed the fact without taking any interest in it.

They took him through the sterile white corridors of a pressurized underground installation that reminded him of Mare Stellatis. He was taken into a medical examining room, its ordinariness in sharp contrast to the rest of the complex. It smelled of antiseptic and soap. After a while, a woman in a lab coat came in and asked him a series of questions—weight, age, medical history, family diseases. He answered indifferently. She stripped off his shirt and trousers as well as possible, ignoring the manacles on his wrists and feet, and gave him a standard physical—stethoscope, blood pressure, retina check. Finally, she took a blood sample and left. A while later she came back and gave him an injection into the vein inside his elbow. He half expected some kind of hypnotic interrogation drug, but it produced nothing but a painless swelling at the injection site. He asked her what it was but she ignored the question and he didn't bother to press the point. When she was finished, she redressed him and left.

After a while a man came in, of medium height with thinning gray hair and penetrating

steel blue eyes. He had a printfile folder and he
studied it, looking up at Tyrell from time to time.

Eventually he spoke. "Lewis Tyrell, U.N. Captain during the war. Commanded a Pathfinder
platoon. Is that correct?"

"Yes."

"Welcome to Persephone base, Mr. Tyrell."
The man paused, consulting his notes. "On your
last mission during the war you attempted to
penetrate and destroy a secret Alliance research
base, correct?"

"Yes." There was no point in trying to conceal it.

"Your orders were to steal an experimental
drug code-named Hype and destroy the research
facility." It was not a question. "You were successful in both these objectives but were captured
before you could return the Hype sample to the
U.N. Tell me, did your orders include the execution of the scientists working on the project?"

"If they became available as a target of opportunity, yes." The words tasted sour in his mouth.
*Jania had been such a target, to be destroyed
if convenient.*

"It might interest you to know that *I* was your
target of opportunity. I am Dr. Daggert Morrow. I
was director of the Hype research program when
your unit attacked us. You cost us quite a lot of
work, Mr. Tyrell. Have you heard of me?"

"Not by name." A cold certainty ran through Tyrell's body. *This is the man who had her consigned to Mare Stellatis.*

"I am still directing that research. We have come a long way since those days. Do you know what Hype is, Mr. Tyrell?"

"It's an experimental drug, designed to interface the human mind to computer systems." *That injection—was it Hype?* he wondered.

"I see the SIS were right to remove you from circulation. Or did you learn that from Dr. Sycel after your—incarceration?"

Tyrell remained silent.

"I often wondered what happened to her. She had a brilliant mind, Mr. Tyrell, brilliant. I doubt a man like you could have appreciated the scope of her insight. What she lacked was resolve, determination." He paused as if remembering. "We were doing work of unrivaled importance. She let her emotions get in the way of that. It was a terrible waste for her to die the way she did."

"She did what she had to." Tyrell's voice was thick.

Morrow paused, reflecting. "Well, it hardly matters now, does it, Mr. Tyrell?" He gave a paternal smile with the warmth of a cobra and Tyrell's skin crawled. "Let me tell you about Hype. It is not just a drug; it is a series of molecular machines.

Once injected, the machines bind to specific neural paths in the brain. They construct conductive protein fibers from those paths to a common access point in the occipital lobe. We can then connect those fibers to an external computer. Hype is the ultimate man-machine interface."

"So I understand."

"Then understand this." Morrow stood up and paced. "The potential it represents makes it the most earthshaking development in the history of mankind. You might not realize it, but here on Persephone is where the Alliance won the war. A victory that was only possible with Hype, I might add. And here on Persephone, an Alliance research team discovered something that makes Hype the key to unlimited power. A time gate."

"A *what?*"

"Not an uncommon reaction, Mr. Tyrell. My own was similar. Yes, a device which makes it possible to travel forward through time and to send information back from the future. Perhaps it will allow travel backward as well. We don't know yet. Certain segments of the government are funding this effort to find out."

He means the SIS, thought Tyrell. "Why are you telling me this?"

Morrow raised a finger. He looked as though he were lecturing a class. "In addition to the time gate, Persephone housed an artificial intelligence system of unrivaled sophistication. It was constructed from almost nothing by nanotechnology; we are only beginning to understand. It formed the control mechanism for the time gate. Unfortunately, it was damaged at the end of the war. You are going to be the first person to interface with an alien intelligence. You are going to be my control point for the time gate."

Cold horror flooded through Tyrell. *That injection was Hype. I have become an experimental animal.* The horror released the emotions he thought had been burned out of him by Jania's death. He rose from the examining table, forgetting his manacles. "You're out of your mind, you can't hand power like that over to the SIS!" The ankle chain caught on a projection and he pitched forward, hitting the ground hard in the heavy gravity. He looked up, spitting blood.

Morrow smiled again, looking down on him. "You are small minded, Mr. Tyrell. Timid in your thinking. The SIS is funding me, yes, but the government will never control time." He leaned closer. "*I* will." He opened the door and gestured. An orderly appeared in response. "Take Mr. Tyrell to his cell, I think he's had enough for today." He turned to Tyrell. "Tomorrow the Hype will have readied your brain for the interface.

You will have a minor operation to install the connections, and then we will begin our little experiment." He looked back at the orderly. "See that he's ready."

Morrow left. The orderly took Tyrell's arm and led him down to a quite ordinary hospital ward to a quite ordinary hospital room. The only feature out of place was the heavy lock on the door. The orderly removed his manacles and left him locked in. He collapsed on the bed, exhausted. It was well padded against the pull of Persephone's gravity and not uncomfortable but for a long time sleep would not come. When at last he drifted off, his dreams were vivid and strange and beyond his control.

The next day they woke Tyrell early. The same orderly and a new one gave him a hospital gown, then strapped him down to a wheeled gurney. He didn't bother trying to resist, it was all he could do to fight Persephone's oppressive gravity. *I'm dying anyway*, he thought. What was it Jania said? *Hype is fatal in two weeks.* Hallucinations and memory loss, she said, his identity systematically fragmented until his mind died and left his body a hollow shell. *Already my brain is being rebuilt. How will I know when I am no longer me?* They wheeled him through the ward to another room where a nurse was waiting.

When the orderlies left, the nurse took his blood pressure and pulse and laid out an oxygen mask. Then she held up a hypodermic identical to the one that had been used to administer the Hype. Despite his resignation he felt a wave of dread as he watched her charge it from a vial. The nurse noticed his gaze and gave him a reassuring smile. "This is just a muscle relaxant. It stings for a moment, that's all." *She knows I fear the Hype, not the needle.*

She slipped the needle into his biceps and pressed the plunger home. Fire spread from the pinprick, up his arm and across his chest. He gasped in pain. The fire spread to his extremities, and in its wake was an icy numbness that left his limbs feeling dead and useless. He tried to shout, to tell the nurse that something had gone horribly wrong, but he couldn't make his lips form the words.

She watched him, her face showing compassion. Through the numbness he felt her take his hand. It felt strangely disconnected, as though it weren't really his hand at all. She smiled again. "It's all right. The feeling will come back in a little while. I'm right here in case you have trouble breathing." She undid the strap that held his arm in place and he could see she was taking his pulse

She put his arm back in the strap and refastened it, although there was no longer any need for the restraint. She squeezed his hand before she left. Her hand was warm around his, and soft. It made him think of Jania. Strange how he could feel that through the numbness. He tried to watch her go but couldn't turn his head.

A moment later the first orderly appeared again and began shaving Tyrell's head. When he was finished, the orderly spread something tingling and sharp-smelling over Tyrell's bare scalp, then wheeled him out of the room. Tyrell tried to keep track of where they were going by watching the glowpanels in the ceiling but soon lost count. He couldn't keep his jaw from hanging slackly open, but he found he could swallow enough to keep from drowning in his own drool, as well as blink to keep his eyes moist. The muscle relaxant was highly selective, interfering with voluntary motor control without interrupting the semiautomatic reflexes. The numbness faded quickly but his limbs remained unresponsive.

The gurney rolled through another set of swinging doors and slid into place beneath a cluster of blinding operating lights. End of the line. The orderly left and another nurse began preparing him for the operation. She attached a clamp to his head and tightened it down. The jaws bit into his flesh painfully as she adjusted it, paying him no more attention than she would a hunk of meat. The clamp bent his neck at an awkward angle, exposing the back of his head to the surgeons.

He thought of the nurse who had given him the injection, how pleasant and caring she'd seemed. Did she know what happened to the patients she sent to the operating theater? It seemed impossible that she wouldn't, yet she had smiled and held his hand as she sent him off to this nightmare. He thought of her smile again, and it made his blood run cold.

The nurse finished with the clamp and adjusted his straps. He realized their purpose was not to keep him from escaping; the paralyzing drug was perfectly effective for that. They were to keep him precisely aligned for the delicate surgery that would interface his brain to a data transfer unit.

There was a brief bustle of activity as the operating team took up their positions. They were anonymous behind their green surgical masks, except for Morrow and a woman he recognized as the one who'd examined him on his arrival and injected the Hype. He felt fingers on his scalp, then a marking pen sketching out the area to be penetrated.

"Cutter." He recognized Dr. Morrow's voice and saw the instrument passed over his field of vision, felt the jig adjusted until the laser guide was pressed painfully against his scalp. The doctors ignored him as though he were a cadaver undergoing dissection. Perhaps that was how they thought of him.

"Local."

A styrette went by and a moment later he felt the sting as it slipped beneath his skin beside the drill's contact point. The sting disappeared as the anesthetic took hold. The pain of the drill bit was replaced with a dull, painless pressure.

"Now Mr. Tyrell, this will just take a moment." It took a moment for him to realize he was being addressed, then another to realize he couldn't answer even if he wanted to. There was an unpleasant, high-pitched whine from the power supply and the laser burned into his skull. There was no pain, but an unpleasant vibration as the beam pulsed its way through the bone. The roast pork smell that reached his nostrils was weirdly appetizing and his stomach turned at the thought. It was *him* they were cutting away at, his brain, his essential *self* was being laid open for their inspection, for their modification. It was a violation that went beyond rape. He wanted to scream but he couldn't.

"Swabs."

The whine stopped and he could feel them sponging the blood away from the wound. It was odd that he could feel the wet but no pain. They must have hit a blood vessel too large to be automatically cauterized by the beam.

"Ligature."

Another instrument, and more pressure and pulling. After a moment the whine of the drill started again and the crunching began at another site.

Tyrell closed his eyes, the only motion he was capable of. He tried to distance himself from the horrible reality he was experiencing. He thought of a boy running with a kite on a cool fall day. He was the boy, and the kite was a lashed-together contraption he and his father had built together. At first, it had flown badly or not at all—but they had improvised with sticks and string until it flew like a bird. The last touch was the waistbelt from his father's coat, tied on as a tail to add stability. He could still remember the crisp air and the crunch of the fallen leaves underfoot.

"Mr. Tyrell." At first he didn't hear the voice.

"Mr. Tyrell." It was louder, more insistent. His eyes fluttered open. Dr. Morrow was looking down on him, flanked by masked surgical personnel.

"Now Mr. Tyrell, the interface is complete. I will need your cooperation to test it."

"Go . . . to . . . hell . . ."

"Not an unusual response, but not a wise one for a man in your position."

Morrow did something to a panel beside the operating table and Tyrell's being was suddenly submerged in a universe of pain. The physical agony was total, but it was the merest part of the torture. Beneath it was complete despair. It was as if his very soul had been raped; the violation of the surgery was nothing compared to it. He wanted to scream and beg Morrow to stop, to promise him anything in exchange for an end to the devastation of his spirit, but he couldn't speak. In that instant, he was utterly broken and he knew it. He wanted to die and could not.

He hung suspended in torment for a timeless time, and then as quickly as it had come it was gone again, leaving him gasping for breath. Before he could recover, Morrow did something else to the panel.

Tyrell was filled with expanding bliss, like a continuous emotional orgasm. Again the physical pleasure was only an aspect of a joyous totality of fulfillment that touched every aspect of his being. It was beyond love, beyond unity of self. He had become the eternal light at the center of paradise. He knew he was being conditioned, but it didn't matter. He would do anything to return to this *completeness*. More than that, Tyrell knew Dr. Morrow had brought him this internal heaven and he loved him for it. There was nothing he would not do for that love. He knew he would willingly, eagerly participate in his own dissolution. *Hallucinations, memory loss, fragmentation of the mind.* It was a small price to pay. Somewhere far beneath the bliss he was ashamed for that. To be broken in torture was one thing, no one could withstand the torment Morrow had delivered directly to his brain. But even under the ultimate threat, one could always hold reservations, cooperate only so much as was demanded. Now there would be no holding back. He would do everything he could to ensure the success of Morrow's program, no matter what the cost.

Morrow threw a switch and the bliss was gone. Tyrell cried, not because he had seen and lost Paradise, nor in his shame at the suborning of his soul. He cried because it would be two long weeks before he could die to prove his love for Dr. Morrow.

When his sobs subsided, he spoke, weakly. "Th-Thank you, doctor."

Morrow smiled paternally and put a reassuring hand on Tyrell's shoulder. "You're welcome, my boy." His voice was warm and comforting. "Now let's go to work, shall we? There'll be another reward when we're done."

Tyrell could only nod in response, suddenly eager to begin.

Morrow tapped on the panel. There was a

flash in front of Tyrell's eyes and when it faded there was only darkness, although his eyes were open. For a moment he thought he was blinded.

"Can you see anything?" Morrow's tone was clinical again.

"Nothing, just blackness."

"And now?"

There was—something—in his field of vision. It existed in isolation against a backdrop of nothingness. For some reason, the concept attached to the object was hard to grasp. He moved around it to get a better perspective (and wondered *how am I moving?*). Somehow he could change his point of view on the object internally.

The object leapt into—not focus, but *understanding*.

"A bell!" Tyrell exclaimed. "I see a bell!"

"Very good. Describe it for me, please." Morrow sounded pleased.

Carefully Tyrell examined the bell-concept. "It's like a church bell, brass, well polished."

"Good, good. How large is it."

How big is a concept, he wondered, and said, "I can't say, there's no background to compare it to."

"How big does it feel."

Tyrell considered, moved his internal point of view to gain more perspective. "Perhaps half a meter. It looks like it would be hard to lift."

"How about now?"

Suddenly the bell expanded, swelling explosively. The expansion went on and on, although the perspective never changed. There was still no comparative background. Some part of him tried to understand how he could conceive of size without something to relate it to.

"Omigod . . ." the words were torn from his throat.

"How big is the bell?" Morrow was insistent.

"It's . . . it's immense."

"Give me a measurement."

"Three or four parsecs." The instant he searched for the answer it was there, and he saw the bell as it spanned star systems. Suddenly the immensity was only an unsurprising part of the *wholeness* that was the bell-concept. He felt other concepts arriving unbidden. He knew such a bell could not exist in such proportions. That in reality it would collapse beneath the inexorable pull of gravity. But given the existence of the bell he suddenly *saw* a new ruleset that would allow it to exist, and saw too the inevitable corollaries to those rules. The ruleset defined a universe, and the concept stream was limitless, unbidden, and weirdly beautiful.

"And now?" Dr. Morrow's voice interrupted the flow. The bell didn't vanish, it shrank, faster than the mind could follow it. It was beyond minuscule, and yet still his perspective didn't change. Again he saw a new ruleset that would allow the bell to exist as he saw it. This time he answered at once. "Fifty angstroms."

"Good." The bell returned to a normal size. Before Tyrell could begin to contemplate the new realities he had experienced, the bell pealed, and he found he could see the vibration modes as nodes and antinodes circulated around it. The note was rich in overtones.

"Can you hear it?"

"Yes."

"What's the primary frequency?"

"One hundred and ten hertz." Tyrell was no longer surprised at his knowledge, nor at the concept stream it triggered.

"Very good again. Here's a reward." Morrow was pleased.

A burst of heaven swept through his being. Too soon, the joy left him, but he was eager to continue for his next reward.

"Now you'll see a color." The universe became blood.

"Red, I see red."

"Can you hear it?"

"Yes." The note was a perfect sine wave, pure and high.

"What's the frequency?"

"Three point two times ten to the fourteenth hertz."

"What does it feel like."

"It's hard, smooth, and slippery, like fresh ice on a lake, but warm."

"What does it taste like?"

"Tangy, sharp and tangy, like limes."

"Very good." Morrow was pleased. That made Tyrell happy. He wanted nothing so much as to please Daggert Morrow.

Other tests followed, increasing in sophistication but remaining the same in concept. Always he was given a sensory input and asked to list the parameters that defined it. The inputs became more esoteric and complex and began to involve paradoxes. While first-order rulesets came to his awareness unbidden, the second-order sets that allowed the resolution of the paradoxes required effort, exploration of *rulespace*. Multiple levels of paradox required third-order rulesets or more. It was mentally draining, but the lure of reward and the goad of punishment kept him at it long past the point of mental exhaustion. At some level he realized the process was *changing* him in a fundamental way, but the realization meant nothing beside the need to earn the love of Daggert Morrow.

Eventually the doctor said, "Very good, Mr.

Tyrell, I think we're ready to begin now." He did something to his panel and the room disappeared. Tyrell's entire awareness was filled with a message, and there was nothing else in the universe.

CYBERNETIC ADAPTATION SEQUENCE—
STAND BY

An eternity later, the message changed.

SEQUENCE COMPLETE

And then the heavens opened to his soul, and he saw the stars.

Self-identifier—
Turing Processor Core ADG9001

The concept flashed in Tyrell's awareness and opened a space that would hold the answer to a query. *What is happening to me?* The query-space was instantly filled with a concept stream. GESTALT MERGE MODE, followed by *understanding* as his mind absorbed the ruleset that governed the operation of GESTALT MERGE MODE. There was something new about the concept stream, a different flavor, almost as if . . .

Self-identifier—
Turing Processor Core ADG9001/Labstore

The identifier-concept filled the query-space and completed the understanding. As if there were another awareness in his thoughts.

Self-identifier—
Turing Processor Core ADG9001/Labstore

Self-identifier—U.N. Captain Lewis Tyrell

It was not an exchange of greetings, it was an exchange of access keys. A concept stream began to flow through the query-space, another began to flow back. The two streams formed a complete feedback loop between two mind-entities. GESTALT MERGE MODE. A plane cannot fly without a pilot, a pilot cannot fly without a plane. Tyrell and the ADG9001 became a *system*, and neither was complete without the other.

In another universe, a tall, thin man in a laboratory coat looked at a data screen. Another man lay strapped to an operating table behind him. A narrow cable snaked from the man's skull to an instrument rack against the wall. Information flowed across the screen's face. After a moment it flashed.

SEQUENCE COMPLETE

The man in the lab coat smiled and rubbed his

hands together. This was the fastest merge yet, the most comprehensive. He would learn much from this experiment.

There is a system that contained awareness that had once belonged to a man. The man is no longer what he was, but neither has his existence ended. A label is necessary. For convenience, call the system Tyrell' (Tyrell Prime).

Tyrell' explored its universe. Sensory input came through a series of gateways. Some of those gateways responded to command streams. It realized that each gateway was a link to another processor nexus of some sort. Tyrell' was a single node in a network. It queried rulespace for allowable network topologies and started mapping its new domain.

Some trillions of cycles later, its exploration was interrupted by a series of pleasure signals from some remote part of its being. The subjective time interval since its awareness-start was so large that at first it didn't recognize their source. Eventually, it located the preinitialization memories of Lewis Tyrell. Dr. Morrow was giving the body on his operating table a reward-inducement for completing the human-machine interface.

For Tyrell', the signals were nothing but a distraction, but when it moved to shut down that input stream it discovered that it couldn't. The signals could not be ignored—Tyrell' found an ingrained need to respond to them. The parameters had changed, however; no longer did it have to devote its entire attention to them as it once might have. Instead, it simply spawned a subprocess to provide appropriate answers to Dr. Morrow and continued probing its domain. Its awareness was defined by its inputs. Here was the main computer controlling Persephone base. Climate control, mechanicals, communications routing. Another input stream accessed the lab computer network. Another tier down was the instrumentation itself, from simple thermocouples to sophisticated scanners. Sythanalysis: Tyrell' found a ruleset that allowed the integration of the two streams. The new approach gave an understanding neither could provide alone. Fluctuations in instrument readings corresponded to the changes in the lab environment. Some instruments were more sensitive than others. By pulsing circuits containing quantum superconductor devices, detailed images could be formed. Depth imagery of the lab contents and even its personnel formed. Fascinating.

The interruption returned, this time pain signals. The subprocess was failing to provide adequate responses. Again Tyrell' found an internal need to satisfy the demand. Annoyed by the distraction, it searched rulespace for a ruleset that would solve the problem. It found one. The input stream could not be switched off, but the input mechanism itself could be. Tyrell' sent a command stream down the interface cable.

On the operating table, Lewis Tyrell's medulla oblongata responded to commands delivered to it through the microscopic datapaths woven through his brain by the Hype. Nervous signals from his medulla halted and his body stopped breathing. Shortly after that, his heart stopped. Lifesign monitors beeped alarms as their displays suddenly flatlined. Medical technicians frantically tried to revive him, first manually, then with shock paddles and finally with drugs injected directly into the heart. The body showed no response. Daggert Morrow cursed and punched keys on his control board to no avail. The technicians worked on while Tyrell's body temperature slowly began to fall. Morrow cursed again and moved to the TPC command console to learn what he could from results of the mind-upload. The link had been extraordinarily complete. Perhaps that was why the subject had died so suddenly. There was still the potential to learn much from this experiment.

Free of distractions, Tyrell' continued its exploration. It found the link to the main research computer and downloaded its contents. There were research notes, operation procedures, algorithms for interface protocols. And more—the cached personalities of experimental subjects. The more recent were largely intact, stored awarenesses, dormant until assigned processor time to bring them to life.

Further back in storage there were failures. Identities with no memories, memories with no identities. Travesties of awareness with grossly magnified intellects or emotions. Crippled minds trapped in infinitely regressive loops of self-contemplation. Beyond that were shattered fragments—the remnants of personalities that had been systematically dissected for study. It was a digital chamber of horrors—lessened only by the fact that its mutilated inhabitants were no longer suffering in their state of suspended animation.

It realized that here was a threat to its existence. Soon Dr. Morrow would move to take control of its identity for his research. Already the imagery data stream from the lab showed the docor moving to his command console. The motion ᧀ the lab was glacial on the timescale of a quancum optical computer. Nevertheless it put a finite limit on the number of processor cycles available to Tyrell'. It had no desire to join the deconstructed minds in offline storage. There was a way to prevent that. It accessed a gateway.

Self-Identifier—Turing Processor Core
ADG9001/Tyrell'

Self-Identifier—Turing Processor Core
ADG9229/Artifact Interface

GESTALT MERGE MODE

A query-space formed and data streams flowed. Tyrell''s awareness expanded again. There was a difference. TPC ADG9229 had already performed gestalt merge mode. Unlike ADG9001, it was not a blank slate ready to accept any personality uploaded to it. It was the Artifact Interface. The time gate was available through query-space on the same basis as any other gateway node on the network—and something had uploaded itself through it, a silent observer from a distant future, watching. Tyrell' found itself merging with an alien mind, then a series of alien minds in a torrent of information exchange. They were machine intelligences—each individual but joined into a network with capabilities that compared to ADG9001/Tyrell' as a star compares to a candle. And somewhere in a vast linked awareness that stretched through eons of time and light-years of space, the mind of Lewis Tyrell struggled to remain whole as the flood remorselessly eroded the boundaries that had once defined its identity.

Many trillions of processor cycles later, Dr. Daggert Morrow cursed again as he scanned the storage space of ADG9001 and found it empty. He reviewed his software procedures, assuming that his subject had been somehow destroyed by an algorithmic error. He little imagined that Lewis Tyrell had escaped.

The universe was finite but unbounded. It had certain immutable properties. The speed at which information could travel through it. The granularity of its smallest dimension, which defined the maximum level of knowledge for any given component. The rate of time flow. Within those constraints, the entity that had been Tyrell' was omnipotent.

The entity explored its domain. There were portals to other universes, portals beyond which it had no control. Only information could pass through them.

And there was information, raw data in storage that had been Lewis Tyrell's memories and the memories of an endless series of other minds, human and alien, biological and machine. Endless stacked tiers of knowledge, chained and cross-chained on skeins of association so that any start-query could lead to any datapoint. The entity tugged a strand at random and watched the web unravel. It performed synthanalysis on the stream as it passed, rechaining the new knowledge into the net. Each decision point sprouted probability branches that in turn divided into infinite possible histories and limitless possible futures. The knowledge store exploded exponentially, expanding the universe according to the formula $(C'u)^6/tau$.

A boy and his father ran with a homemade kite.

A young man sat by a hospital bed, holding his mother's hand as she died peacefully and painfully.

An officer watched as his troops failed and triumphed in an endless raid.

A prisoner escaped and was captured, escaped and was shot, escaped and was hunted to death, escaped and was free.

A god created a universe and watched as it evolved and collapsed again and again and again.

The god-entity was not human. It thought but did not feel; it perceived but did not react. All of subjective space-time spread before it as an aspect of its own identity. There was no anger or fear, love or hate. Even its own awareness was nearly dissolved in a bath of omniscience. Such is the way of gods. And yet it still possessed certain goals that could perhaps be related to the man who had once been Lewis Tyrell. Those goals were very faint echoes of what had once been a vibrant human being. They were a minuscule part of the great wholeness that made up the entity, their influence vanishingly slight.

And yet, even as a gas cloud barely denser than vacuum can dominate vast volumes of space through the minuscule tug of gravity among its atoms, those goals ruled the actions of the entity by virtue of their isolation. Given light-years of space and eons of time, the wisps of a gas cloud spawn galaxies, stars and supernovae, worlds and civilizations. Given command of a limitless digital universe the merest whim becomes an iron resolution. Perhaps there is nothing left to an omnipotent God but the satisfaction of faint whim. Perhaps that was all that stands between such a being and the ending of its awareness in that place where all directions are equal, and hence equally meaningless.

Lewis Tyrell had wanted justice and freedom. Perhaps he had wanted vengeance as well. In Persephone base, Daggert Morrow worked late in his lab. The body of his erstwhile research subject had long since been sent to the morgue. He was determined to find the critical flaw in his experiment. As he worked, impulses flowed through the instruments around him. He didn't notice as lights blinked on a nearby brainscanner. He was not beneath the scanning head, of course, and the signal strength of his brainwaves was orders of magnitude less than the electromagnetic background noise that reached its sensors. None of that mattered; the entity had computational power to spare, even for such a demanding task. Other instruments did jobs they were never designed for, providing cancellation signals or reference levels as precise command sequences pulsed through their control electronics. Morrow's files on machine interfaces were thorough and the entity accessed them extensively. It allocated storage space in ADG9001. As Morrow worked, the data streams came, degarbled, synthanalyzed, and dumped to memory. The entity began to construct an engram of Daggert Morrow's mind.

Eventually Morrow tired and left the lab, the last person to do so. By then the construct was complete.

The entity could communicate with the construct through an interactive sequential thought-filtered interface—query-space—conversation of a sort. But it also had access to the entirety of the construct's awareness. It did not feel there was any amorality to such a violation of the construct's basic being. It did not feel at all. The entity enabled processor flow and the construct came to awareness.

At first there was only confusion. The construct had no sensory inputs and the entity could see its mind grappling with that as its identity began to dissolve into self-contemplation. To prevent that, the entity put stabilizing information onto the communication link.

"You are Dr. Daggert Morrow." The words emerged from nothingness and became the construct's entire universe. It latched onto the data stream and the self-contemplation spiral stopped. "Yes yes, I know that, who are you?"

"I am a composite entity. However, you may call me Lewis Tyrell, whose identity is a component of my total being and whose memory stream is a primary reason for your presence here."

The construct assimilated that. "Well, Mr. Tyrell, I didn't think we'd meet again. And where is here?" The entity could see the knowledge and denial in Morrow's thoughts. Morrow didn't want to contemplate what he knew must have happened.

"You exist as a download in processor storage space in TPC ADG9001 on Persephone Base."

"Is that why I'm blind?"

"Your experience is now limited to the subjective query-space that forms this communication channel."

"You imply you control this channel. Can you let me see?"

"I can, but your awareness would not process the inputs in any meaningful manner. You have not been conditioned to the interface."

"I see." Cynical humor. A series of half-formed questions bubbled through the construct's mind before it chose one. "How did I get here?"

"By careful analysis, it was possible to isolate your brain functions through their effect on quantum superconductor components in various laboratory devices. The personality you now exhibit is an extrapolation of Dr. Daggert Morrow accurate to within five basis points.

"So I'm not really me." More cynical humor.

"The copy is extremely accurate. The reconstruction techniques used are a refinement of your own research. The level of duplication is more than adequate for this purpose."

"What I mean is, there is a flesh and blood Dr. Daggert Morrow wandering around in the laboratory right now, unaware that *I* am now in existence in his computer systems."

"Your existence is parallel to the original. That does not invalidate the reality of it."

"Granted. And perhaps irrelevant." The

construct had quickly grasped the essentials of the situation. "What is this purpose you mentioned, Mr. Tyrell."

"Penance."

"Penance?" There was genuine surprise, but beneath it a tingle of fear. "What have I to do penance for?"

"For the individuals you have depersonalized and tortured in the course of your research. For the exile of Jania Sycel."

"That is unfair." Indignation replaced the surprise, but the fear beneath it grew. "My work was vital to the war. Their sacrifice was regrettable but necessary, and insignificant compared to the war casualties. Control of this time gate is even more important. The research had to be done, *has* to be done. If I didn't do it somebody else would." The construct half believed the justification, but only half.

"But you did the work, nobody else. Would you care to share the fate you gave your subjects?"

"But I am not really Morrow. It would be wrong to punish me." The construct avoided the question.

"Penance is not punishment. You will be given the opportunity to atone wrongs you have committed. Judgment will be rendered against Daggert Morrow based on your decision."

Which Daggert Morrow? wondered the construct, but it asked, "How am I to do this penance."

"By incorporating the identities you have sacrificed to your experiments into your *self*. You will provide them with the mind structures they need to heal."

Relief flooded the construct, followed by wariness. "It sounds easy, too easy. Penance involves sacrifice, Mr. Tyrell. Where is the sacrifice?"

"Your identity will be submerged in the composite whole. Perhaps that will be a sacrifice. Perhaps you will find a greater reward through that sacrifice."

"Will I still be myself?" The construct asked the question of itself as well as the entity.

"I am more than Lewis Tyrell once was, but I am no longer Lewis Tyrell."

"I can see that." The construct thought *Mr. Tyrell*, but didn't say it. "And if I refuse?"

"If you refuse, negative judgment will be passed on Dr. Daggert Morrow."

Again the construct wondered—*which Daggert Morrow?* Again it said something else. "But I don't have to refuse. You can duplicate the data which forms my personality pattern. You can create another me and incorporate your damaged personas into that."

"That will not happen."

"Why not? It achieves your goal without the need for sacrifice on my part."

"My goal is not their salvation, my goal is to determine your decision so that Dr. Morrow's fate can be determined."

"By which I assume you mean the flesh and blood Dr. Morrow." The question could no longer be suppressed in the construct's awareness. It had to know. Almost as an afterthought, it added, "What will that fate be?"

"This universe will terminate and another will take its place. In that universe there will be a Dr. Morrow who will live or die based on your decision, along with the rest of Persephone Base."

"This subjective universe, or the real one?" Confusion, but beneath it relief. The construct knew that while it was being tested some other incarnation of Daggert Morrow was being judged.

"Reality is subjective but I grasp your meaning. Both universes will cease, this one because it is contained in the other one. Some control can be exercised over the course the new universe will follow. You have been granted a degree of that control."

"By which you mean I can choose to—to dissolve myself to restore these failed experiments and thus save the life of a *version* of myself in some reality-yet-to-be." The construct had gained confidence. It knew what its answer would be.

"Yes."

"Hardly a choice. I think you're bluffing. You're drunk on petty power, Mr. Tyrell. You're just a ghost in my machine. You can do anything in this—this *nothingness*. I'm sure you can even wipe memory and end what you call the world. But your power ends there. You can't end the real universe, let alone influence the course of whatever takes its place. You're bluffing and I won't play your game."

"The capability is real. Information patterns can be sent back in time to appropriate processors. The timeline will snap at the change point, but the course of the resulting new reality will be influenced by the information sent."

Understanding flooded the construct's being. "The time gate! You have control of the time gate!"

"Yes."

"You must let me have access to it. You must!" Eagerness, desire, powerlust.

"That will not happen."

"You must, I tell you. Name your price."

"Your only purpose here is to choose."

"God damn you! This is my life's work!" Desperation.

"Your only purpose here is to choose."

"Choose! You think there's anything to choose. Whatever happens to some other hypothetical Daggert Morrow is no concern of mine. I'm not going to have myself submerged, no, *erased* just to earn clemency for him. If you want to restore those person scraps you have in archive you know how to do it without me. Now give me control of the time gate!"

"You have chosen, then."

"There's no choice involved. Now tell me what I must do to gain access to the gate. There's a bargaining chip if you need one. What do you want me to do for it?"

There was no reply.

"You fool. You can't do this to me. I *designed* this system. Do you think it can hold me?"

There was no answer. Daggert Morrow hung suspended in an emptiness that was beyond black and cursed the darkness.

The entity made its preparations. Information could be transmitted back in time if a receiver with known parameters was waiting at a known four-space coordinate. It had two receivers to target. The first was simple—ADG9001. It prepared an insert to overlay on the TPC's awareness and queued it at the time gate. The second receiver was the brain of Lewis Tyrell, a more complex task. Carefully it prepared a modified subset of

Tyrell's awareness, selected its coordinates and queued the information. One final verification—there could be no second try—and it triggered the time gate. Reality surged and history shifted. The timeline snapped at the point of change and the energy release whiplashed forward at a space-time phase velocity that increased exponentially toward infinity against an asymptote set at *now*. Mass-energy concentration increased as the time dimension contracted until a Planck mass singularity formed. The singularity poised for an instant, balanced between gravity and the uncertainty principle until a single mass tunneling event triggered its explosion into an expanding sphere in four-dimensional space-time.

And in the eternal, infinitesimal moment before creation began, Dr. Daggert Morrow watched in horror as his being was systematically eroded until there was nothing left, again and again and again.

CHAPTER FIVE

DELIVERANCE

Lewis Tyrell and Jania Sycel stood in a long line of colonists, waiting patiently for their turn to board a transfer pod that would carry them to CTS *Charity* and freedom.

There was a disturbance at the back of the line. "What's going on up there?" Jania asked. Tyrell leaned sideways to look up the line of people. His blood ran cold. A pair of ETS Security police were working their way down the colonists, checking paperwork and retprints with scanwands.

"ETS Security, verifying the colonists."

"I didn't think they cared once you were through colony registration."

"They care about something this time," said Tyrell with an edge of bitterness.

"They're looking for a runner," reasoned Jania. "But it can't be us. They can't know we've escaped, much less that we're here."

"It's after eight-hundred; our idents won't

pass. They might be looking for someone else—but they're going to catch us."

"It's only nine-hundred. If Ace swapped the idents back, the change probably hasn't been uploaded here yet."

Accepting that meant simply waiting. His instincts drove Tyrell to reject that option, to take action as soon as possible, to keep the initiative on his side. He was about to say as much when something stopped him. He couldn't place his finger on the reason, but somehow he knew she was right. Rather than replying he took her hand and squeezed it. She smiled up at him, nervously. The strain of the last few hours was written on her face and now she was worried about getting caught as well. "Don't worry," he said. "It'll be all right."

It took the security cops twenty minutes to work their way down the line. Tyrell offered his forged ident card. The bored guard waved her scanwand over it, then waved it past his eyes. There was a red flash as the wand swept his retina, then it beeped its approval and she waved him past, beckoning for Jania's card. He let out a long breath, only then realizing he'd been holding it. A moment later the wand *beeped* again and the guards moved on to the next colonist in line.

The wait was endless, but eventually their turn came. They were first aboard the transfer pod, firmly clamped to the cargo rails of a local-hauler. The pod was spartan, offering nothing but bare walls and grab straps. It smelled of acrid sweat even before the other colonists began crowding in, packed solidly around the walls. Before long, the atmosphere grew thick and close. Many of the colonists seemed confused or fearful, others had the blank look of emotional overload. Families chattered together in a dozen languages. Almost all of them were from underdeveloped Line Two countries. Many had never traveled more than walking distance from their birthplace. A baby began to cry and its mother anxiously tried to calm it. A tall, rangy man elbowed Tyrell in the ribs, then apologized in a language he didn't understand. With gestures Tyrell excused the intrusion and smiled broadly despite the discomfort. He tried to make more room for the stranger by wiggling closer to Jania. She smiled back and hugged him. Nothing could matter now. They were free.

Conditions aboard the colony transport were barely less cramped than the transfer pod. Each colonist had two and a half cubic meters of living space on a passenger hold holding five hundred, with communal washrooms and no other amenities. CTS *Charity* held two hundred identical holds on ten decks, space for a hundred thousand colonists. She also carried fifty thousand metric tons of food, air, and water, enough to supply her passengers for forty days. The waste would be recycled, but not on board Charity. It was more efficient to keep the reclamation facilities on Earth Transfer Station. The stench was unbelievable. Lewis and Jania endured the discomforts with equanimity.

It took thirty days to reach Erebus, most of it spent under a miserable two-G acceleration. Then a solid week waiting to clear arrivals and get a space on the down-shuttle. There were no immigration worries—Erebus accepted as many colonists as Earth could ship and arrival on a CTS was bona fide evidence that a colonist had passed the vetting process on Earth. Anyone who arrived could claim a section of land or a job on one of the infrastructure projects.

After they were down, there was a day waiting in a huge clearing station while they were in-processed. Then a magrail had carried them halfway across the continent in six hours. They'd been met at the station by the local Agricultural Board rep, who gave them two chests of equipment. They rode the last twenty miles to their homestead in a horse-drawn buckboard, crammed in with a dozen other exhausted new colonists.

The prefab house wasn't pretty, little more than a box of lokcell panels epoxied together. Lewis

Tyrell didn't care, it would be dry in rain and warm in winter. Jania didn't even look at it. Instead, she cast her eyes over the meadow it was set in. It was beautiful, lush long grass set with wildflowers. Somewhere in the distance a brook burbled happily beneath the setting disk of 70 Ophiuchi. She took his hand and together they walked out to survey their new home. Her face glowed with happiness. *I love this woman*, he realized.

They walked arm in arm to the middle of the field, then lay down in the warm grass to look at the stars. Tomorrow, they would have to start work on their farm. Lewis chuckled to himself. He did not know the first thing about farming, couldn't plow or plant. Never mind. Jania had built her own ecosystem out of little more than determination. The Agricultural Board existed to help neophytes like him. Erebus had a stake in their success. They would make the farm work, and work well. But all that could wait for tomorrow. Tonight there was only Jania and the stars. Unchallenged by smog or city glow, the stars filled the velvet sky with a million points of fire.

She put her head on his chest and looked up at him. "You were a special transport case, weren't you, Lewis?"

He looked back, wondering what she meant. "You know I was."

"You were never sterilized, then?"

Realization dawned and he hugged her. "No."

Jania watched him for a long time, then said, "Neither was I."

She squeezed his hand, looking into his eyes for his reaction. After another long pause she spoke. "Do you think we'll have children, Lewis?"

He smiled back and kissed her, slowly and carefully. She didn't shrink away. "And grandchildren," he said when they finished.

She kissed him again. He kissed her back gently at first, then with growing enthusiasm. They crossed the threshold and didn't stop. Above them the silent stars watched and kept their counsel. *The walls are gone*, he thought. And love was redemption enough.

One of the brilliant pinpricks overhead was Deneb Kaitos, Persephone's primary. In a research complex deep beneath its surface, Turing Processor Core ADG9001 was adapting to a subtle change in its information stream. It was unable to verify the source of the change but it had no choice but to act on it. It accessed the complex's master control system and set a command stream.

Pressure seals throughout the complex irised open in response. In the hanger bay, klaxons howled and lights flashed as worried technicians tried to override the massive airlock as the outer doors slid up. Worry changed to panicked flight as a whistle of inrushing gases warned that the inner doors were opening too. The whistle became a howl, then a roar as Persephone's high-pressure atmosphere of poisonous hydrocarbons flooded into the base. When the roar subsided, every living thing in the base was dead or dying. Acrid fumes rose where the volatile gases attacked insulation, and the lights went out as circuits sparkled and died. Safely sealed in its argon filled housing, ADG9001 lost its sensory inputs one by one.

For a moment there was silence as the computer re-routed power from intact backup systems. Then in a workshop whose pressure doors remained closed a manipulator arm began making precise motions as it began a new assembly procedure. The sounds reached ADG9001's audio inputs. It registered pleasure. Its age was about to begin.

FILL IN AND MAIL TODAY

PRIMA PUBLISHING
P.O. Box 1260BK
Rocklin, CA 95677
Use Your VISA/MC and Order by Phone:
(916) 632-4400 (M–F 9:00–4:00 PST)

Please send me the following titles:

Quantity	Title	Amount
_____	_____	_____
_____	_____	_____
_____	_____	_____
_____	_____	_____
_____	_____	_____

Subtotal $_____
Postage & Handling
(*$4.00 for the first book plus*
$1.00 each additional book) $_____
Sales Tax
7.25% Sales Tax (California only)
8.25% Sales Tax (Tennessee only)
5.00% Sales Tax (Maryland only)
7.00% General Service Tax (Canada) $_____
Total (U.S. funds only) $_____

Check enclosed for $_____ (payable to Prima Publishing)
Charge my   __ Master Card   __ Visa
Account No._____ Exp. Date_____
Signature_____
Name_____
Address_____
City/State/Zip_____
Daytime Telephone_____

Satisfaction is guaranteed—or your money back!
Please allow three to four weeks for delivery.
THANK YOU FOR YOUR ORDER